ONE HUNDRED DAYS

One Hundred Days

Lukas Bärfuss

Translated from the German by
Tess Lewis

GRANTA

The author wishes to thank the Pro Helvetia foundation and the canton of Zürich for their support with this work

Granta Publications, 12 Addison Avenue, London W11 4QR
First published in Great Britain by Granta Books 2012

Copyright © Wallstein Verlag, Göttingen 2008
Translation © 2012 Tess Lewis

Originally published in German as *Hundert Tage* in 2008 by
Wallstein Verlag, Göttingen

The right of Lukas Bärfuss to be identified as the author of this work and
Tess Lewis's right to be identified as its translator have been asserted by
them in accordance with the Copyright, Designs and Patents Act 1988

The translation costs of this book were supported by a grant from Pro Helvetia

swiss arts council
prohelvetia

A CIP catalogue record for this book is available from the British Library

9 8 7 6 5 4 3 2 1

ISBN 978 1 84708 480 4

www.grantabooks.com

Typeset by Avon DataSet, Bidford on Avon, Warwickshire

Printed and bound by CPI Group (UK) Ltd, Croydon, CR0 4YY

For Kaa, always

Is this what a broken man looks like, I wonder, as I sit across from him in the afternoon and outside the snow we had been expecting for days finally starts to fall in delicate flakes onto the brownish green fields. It's hard to say exactly what in him is broken, certainly not his backbone. He sits up straight, chooses his words deliberately, without haste, and seems almost relaxed. Only the way he raises the cup to his lips, slowly, a touch too slowly, too controlled, might offer a hint of his inner devastation. Maybe he's worried that spilling even a single drop might be enough to upset his equilibrium. I know I don't need to speculate, because he *is* a broken man, he must be, after all he has told me and, even more importantly, all that he hasn't.

Occasionally he pauses while speaking, often in the middle of a sentence. I can see in his eyes how he remembers, just remembers and doesn't speak, maybe because he doesn't have the words, hasn't found them yet and probably never will. It seems as if his eyes are following the events, those events that took place in Amsar House, where he spent the hundred days. The most surprising part of this story is that he was the one who had lived through it, he who had seemed destined to suffer nothing more than the usual dose of human catastrophe: a nasty divorce, a serious illness, at the very most a house fire. He certainly didn't seem like someone who would end up in the middle of a crime of the century. Not this man, not David Hohl, who went to

I

school with me and in whom I can still see the lanky boy with the slightly pendulous lower lip from which a thread of saliva seemed about to drip whenever something amazed him, but of course never actually did fall. His lip was just always a bit moist and merely showed more clearly than others' did exactly what lips are, namely the inside of the mouth turned outward.

As a child, he was no daredevil. He rarely risked trouble, not because he was a coward but because most adventures and dares just didn't seem worth the bother to him. He was completely level-headed, except for three or four episodes, but they don't really count since they were so rare. Besides, people only remember the last one, when David suddenly became pale and ominously still, then flushed red and choked out a few curses before ranting about the injustice of the world in words no one would ever have expected from a boy of ten or eleven. He had, to put it mildly, a highly developed sense of justice, which wasn't tied to the rationality that was his other main characteristic, nor was it the product of a carefully considered world view. No, it was pure feeling, an emotional response. I remember how he once let a few boys from the upper grades beat the living daylights out of him, just because he overheard them running down another student and confronted them since, in his view, this was just not acceptable. After the break, he sat down at his desk with a bloody nose, and when the teacher told him to go to the washroom, he refused to get up and said that he wasn't ashamed of his injury.

We had no idea what drove him, but assumed he wanted to impress everyone, especially the girls, with his heroic championing of just causes. It was unsettling to see how well it worked, and that's why we considered him a bit mad, although not a complete lunatic. Perhaps it was this particular character trait that landed

2

him in his later difficulties, and I ask him if he thought of himself as a defender of justice. He smiles and takes a sip of coffee before answering, speaking like someone admitting to an earlier belief in flying saucers or the existence of Atlantis.

I believed in good. I wanted to help people, like everyone in the agency, and not just to lift individuals out of misery, but to help all of mankind. For us, the idea of development was not just economic development, building streets, or reforestation. For us it was the development of human awareness of universal justice.

But that doesn't explain why you stayed, I dare to object, why you didn't leave with the others when it was clear the situation would end in a bloodbath.

He looks out at the flurries of snow, each flake a thought, and says, It wasn't so clear to me at the time. And I wanted to stay with Agathe, but sometimes I think I stayed only because of Paul's shoes, his hiking boots with red laces and a deep tread, waxed boots that could take you anywhere, to the highest peaks and through the deepest canyons. All those years, little Paul had only worn sandals. True, they were sturdy, with thick soles, but still, they were just sandals and they showed, in their way, the depth of his trust in that country. No one, not even his feet, had anything to fear. And three days before our evacuation, Paul suddenly appeared wearing hiking boots that were intended to get him out of the country safe and sound. And I was ashamed at the thought that all those years he had kept a pair of carefully waxed boots in his house for just such an emergency. We acted as if the events had been unforeseeable, as if Hell had broken loose, completely out of the blue, but that little man, my direct superior, had his boots. He was prepared. He saw it coming. He knew that one day sandals would no longer be enough and he got himself a pair of hiking boots. For me this was a betrayal. The calculation evident in his choice of footwear, his strategy in the middle of this chaos – which, by the way, only appeared chaotic, was meant to appear chaotic, but in reality was a meticulously organized Hell, well thought-out, prepared, and executed – his calculation offended my sense of honor. I didn't want to be a coward in good shoes, and when the moment came, after I'd bolted the door of Amsar House and was about to leave for the embassy, where the others were already waiting, I went around to the back of the house, slipped in behind the emergency generator and didn't move. The convoy was scheduled to leave Kigali for Bujumbara at noon. All I had to do was hold out for a few hours. They wouldn't be able to wait; things had got too hot. I huddled in the small recess with a bottle of water and a box of cheese crackers, and at some point, someone came looking. He called my name and a buzzard almost blew my cover when it sat on the generator and started screeching, but I didn't move. A few minutes later, I heard steps receding along the gravel path. Then I was alone. Isn't it amazing how simple it is to hide, how simple and effective?

Outside the window, the flakes fall more heavily, the dark fields are powdered here and there with white, like a warm cake sprinkled with icing sugar. This is a miserable place, David says, but no more miserable than others. At least here everyone isn't stepping on each other's toes. And his comment answers a question I had been asking myself for a while: why did he move here, of all places, to the damp, raw climate of the Jura mountains, where the winters are hard and snowy? For several years he had wandered throughout Switzerland, he told me, looking for a place he could live in peace, but after a few months he always moved on, from one furnished room to the next. And now he's here, in a long

4

valley filled with dark fir trees, over which the continental winds blow without drawing up the frigid air that sinks onto the land like a cold reservoir, a refrigerator one kilometer square.

I waited until it was dark and then I slipped into Amsar House. We had boarded up the windows of our houses, but I left the boards for the time being and started to draw up an inventory. I didn't own much that was useful in the situation. I had barely any water, a few cans of Heinz baked beans, a half dozen candles, matches, that was it. Still, I wasn't worried. I just had to hold out for a few days, until I found Agathe, then everything would work out. I wanted her to see that she was wrong, that I hadn't run off as she'd always predicted I would. One day, the big white machine will come, like an angel in the sky, it will appear and will carry you all away – that's what she said. But after that first night, I was terrified. I realized my mistake and all I wanted was to get out of Kigali. I knew there was an Air France flight the following Sunday to evacuate the last Europeans, and I would be sitting on that plane – with Agathe. I'd had my gardener Théoneste take a message to her house on Avenue de la Jeunesse. I started packing. I knew she would come. This nightmare would just be an episode in our life, which we'd joke about soon enough. But she didn't come. And I stayed in Amsar House; I stayed there for one hundred days, and sometimes it's as if I'm still sitting within those walls, and the fear washes over me again. I hear screams and the sounds of war and I feel the pangs of hunger again and the thirst.

Every few days, Théoneste brought me water, a bit of cooked rice and occasionally a bottle of beer. He was good to me, even if he wasn't good to others, but I knew nothing of that at the time. We played *tufi* on the veranda. He brought news of developments on the front lines, about streams of refugees, and now and again a rumor: that Agathe had left the city, say, or was treating the wounded in a military camp – the gossip changed from day to day. Only one thing was certain: her house, her family's home, had been hit by a grenade one of the very first days of April, but no one knew if there had been any casualties.

Refugees from the north were living in the ruins, and when I climbed up onto the roof during the day, I could see the rebel positions on the other side of the Nyabugogo swamps. Every day they drew nearer. The government troops only controlled the central hill with the police station, the military camp, and the ministries, and it was clear they couldn't hold Kigali. The transitional government had abandoned the capital a few days after the presidential aircraft was shot down, so there wasn't, strictly speaking, anything left for the troops to defend. They only held their position so that the militias could continue their work.

At this point, David falls silent and looks around his apartment as if, any minute, he expects someone to emerge from the darkness that thickens around us.

But I had other problems. Sometimes Théoneste didn't come for days at a time, and then only brought a small bowl of rice, a few dried beans that I had to soak until they were soft enough to eat raw. I set out pans in the garden to gather rainwater – even though in those days it wasn't a good idea to go out of the house. Not good at all. It smelled like the collection point for dead animals in the Lerchenfeld district, you remember, where we had to bring dead cats or cows that didn't survive the birth of their first calf. That's what it smelled like, but the stench was unbelievably strong, as if you were sitting right in one of those containers where they put the dead animals. At first I couldn't take it for more than a minute without vomiting. You could even smell it in the house, and I had to force myself to drink the rainwater. I'd heard about corpses being washed down the Nyabarango River and I couldn't get rid of the idea that the water of which we humans are mostly constituted could evaporate along with the river water. Some of the rain must have been made up of water from those corpses and I'd have given anything to be able to boil it before drinking.

Still, the hunger and the thirst weren't the worst part. The worst was the darkness, the night that fell over the land every evening at exactly six o'clock and covered me almost like a physical object, like a blanket or a stream of tar. If I had been a traveler looking for shelter in the night, I would have had to use the stars to find my way, by following Procyon in Canis Minor, or Ras Alhague in the Serpent-Bearer constellation. I wasn't very economical. I quickly burned through my supply of candles and had to spend the nights in pitch darkness. I felt like I was dropped into a barrel of black ink every night and when the sun rose on the horizon twelve hours later, as regular as an alarm clock, I was left behind like a black stain, a walking glob of tar. I didn't dare look in the mirror. I was worried the darkness might have stuck to me, like soot under a miner's eyes when he crawls out of the shaft at the end of his shift.

We're not made for those nights, me and everyone else in the agency. We come from the zone of twilight. We need transitions, periods of half-light. We're attuned to the rhythms of light that accompany our lives, the muted early autumn sunlight, or the sharp April shadows. At our latitude, we can never be certain at any given time if it's still morning or if noon has already arrived. When does night begin and when does it end? We live in a realm of approximation, but there, two degrees south of the equator, the sun doesn't offer any leeway. Night falls like a guillotine, without the slightest hint of twilight. A barely noticeable lurch of the sun heralds the end of the day. Nature flips the switch. She never grants a moment's delay nor any half measures so that you might play for just a minute in the evening light. From the very first instant there is complete, absolute darkness and that's what wears down the Europeans. Sometimes I felt as if I were lying in the center of the earth, as if I were sitting inside some stinking monstrosity that burped every now and again or explosively farted out the gasses escaping from the entangled corpses. The sound of fighting at night didn't worry me; on the contrary, it was familiar. After all, we grew up with it, didn't we? David says, and he stands up. Like David, I remember watching endless columns of tanks passing along the road towards the mountain and hearing the thunder of the howitzers and the rattling of machine-guns from the drill ground. When you grow up in a garrison town, as David and I did, you get your toys from the armory – 102-volt radio batteries that we would tape together and throw in the midst of a school of minnows. The fish floated on their backs for a moment and we flipped them onto land, where they revived and trembled helplessly until little bits of gravel stuck to their silvery stomachs. We never knew what to do with our catch. The minnows were too small to eat. Sometimes we went at them with our pocket-knives. We pressed down until their intestines spurted out of their bodies. Other times, we magnanimously threw them back in the water.

David goes to turn the burner on under a casserole and sets the table while he waits for our meal to heat up. The small bulb in the cooker hood, yellowed by a layer of grease, provides the only light in the room. Outside the world has turned blue as the snow continues to fall. A layer of snow coats the windowsill like white fleece. As David ladles our dinner into bowls I see he's serving tripe prepared by the butcher – the best tripe he's ever eaten, he declares, as he attacks his helping with an almost indecent appetite. After all he's been through, I expected him to have become a vegetarian, but not only does he eat meat, he even eats entrails, like beef tripe. I wonder if he's making a statement, trying to tell me something about his constitution, perhaps, to prove he's unscathed by the whole ordeal, that, no matter how horrible it was, it isn't going to keep him from eating intestines with red sauce.

No, David resumes, after wiping his mouth, the sounds of war never bothered me, only the shouting of the militia was bad. From sun-up to sun-down you could hear them bellowing on Avenue des Grands Lacs, where they had set up a roadblock, and they always played those stupid Simon Bikindis songs, carrying out their work to the constant, unchanging rhythm as long as there was enough light to see. Because as soon as it got dark, they fled into their houses and left the streets to the regular troops. The murderers were afraid of the dark – that's the subtle humor that Kigali had to offer in those days.

At first I kept the shutters closed during the day, but then Théoneste told me that the militia knew that an *umuzungu*, a white man, was stranded in Amsar House. He had told them I was Swiss and so was on their side. If I were Belgian, they'd have killed me without a second thought. But these murderers, who killed anyone with an identity card that had the wrong ethnicity boxes checked under *ubwoko*, these murderers considered me an ally, a collaborator, like all the Swiss over the past thirty years, since we first arrived in that country. Why should anything have changed just because they were hacking off women's breasts and

9

cutting unborn children out of their mothers' bodies? After all, we were the ones who taught them administration and how to take on projects of this scale. The logistics are the same whether you're moving bricks or corpses. Yes, the militias left me in peace.

I don't know if I ever really loved Agathe. Maybe in the four years I knew her, I was just trying to forget our first meeting, to wash away the injury she inflicted on me in Brussels airport. I wanted her to know that I wasn't the stupid kid she took me for when I stood up for her at passport control.

It was my very first time on an airplane, late June, 1990. I was on my way to my posting at the agency's office in Kigali. They were expecting me and I was told it would take a considerable amount of work to clear up the mess my predecessor had left behind. I was traveling on an official mission. I felt important. Because I was coming from Zurich, I had to get off the Sabena aircraft and go through Belgian passport control. There she was: an African woman in European clothes, wearing capris that showed off her slender ankles, open-toed shoes and red-painted toenails. This was not a sight I'd seen very often. Under her arm, she carried a funny umbrella with a handle shaped like a duck's head. There was a problem with her papers – that is, her passport was valid but, as I learned later, the problem was her nationality. The Belgian immigration officers were harassing her just because she was a citizen of a former colony. They kept leafing through her papers, asking intrusive questions. One of the two, the one with thicker bands of braid on his uniform and a drinker's complexion, disappeared for a long time. The people waiting behind us had long since moved to other queues. I was the only one who hadn't, and I remained there because I wasn't going to abandon the woman to these monsters. She herself stayed calm and let it all wash over her, but I got angrier with each passing minute. Just as I was wondering whether or not I should stay behind the yellow line as the worn markings on the floor indicated, the immigration officer uttered a vile expression used by the Portuguese slave-traders. I'd first learned its meaning and origin less than a month before my departure in the intercultural communications module of my training course. It was an insult based on skin color.

I could picture the three skull and crossbones on our worksheets used to flag words that were completely prohibited from the vocabulary of employees of the Swiss Agency for Development and Cooperation.

That was my *casus belli*. The yellow line was my Rubicon and I crossed it right then, without the slightest hesitation. I was going to make it clear to those racist idiots that a new time had come. After three decades, these scoundrels in their gray uniforms still hadn't got over the loss of their colonies. I'd heard about the museum in Tervuren, just outside Brussels, built by Leopold II, the father of all racist scoundrels. The museum shamelessly paid homage to the crimes committed by the Force Publique, presented that assassin Stanley as a great man and displayed the trunks from his voyage in the Congo like a hero's reliquaries. So be it, but they had to realize that the world's conscience had turned against them. I'm afraid I aimed a few curses in our mother tongue in their direction.

A moment later, two security officers I hadn't noticed before grabbed me and lifted me off the ground. This not only hurt, but it drained my *joie de vivre* for the next few days, even weeks, and almost jeopardized my mission. To be honest, what cast a shadow over my four years in Kigali wasn't this rude treatment nor the brutality with which they dragged me to some remote corner of the airport – it was the beautiful African woman's face. I had got myself into trouble because of her lightly freckled nose, her light gray eyes and eyebrows arched like two bass clefs. I didn't look at her face for more than a second, and for the first quarter of that second I couldn't read the expression in her eyes. Her gaze was just as indifferent as before. In the next quarter of a second a smile spread across her face, proud and full of contempt for the world, which encouraged me and gave me strength. I wanted to make her understand with a single glance that she didn't need to worry, even if they were taking me to the hangman. The defense of human dignity would be worth ten times the sacrifice.

But I misunderstood something in her expression, because the last fraction of the second revealed what the woman was really thinking. Her contempt wasn't directed at the world, only at me. And to make this perfectly clear, she pressed her tongue against her upper teeth, made a vacuum against her palate and let the air rush in, making the clicking noise that is the international sound of disapproval. She took *me* for the idiot, not the two immigration officials, who were also smirking and sneering at me as if I were a complete imbecile. Even the duck's head on her umbrella mocked me. Then the security officers dragged me past the gaping travelers and through the security barrier.

They threw me into a cell the size of a handkerchief, a room with a table and two chairs. I was so agitated, sweat was pouring off me. I'd never experienced a greater injustice in my life. On top of that, my suitcase was gone. But once I'd calmed down a bit, I told myself that it would surely all be cleared up soon. I wasn't just any traveler. I was an employee of the Federal Department of Foreign Affairs, of the agency's head office, an administrator on official business. And I had time. My connecting flight didn't leave for two hours.

But no one came to whom I could explain the situation. No official appeared, not after one hour, not after an hour and a half. Only at the very moment that my plane was scheduled to take off, and so, of course, was leaving without me, did I notice there was no lock on the door. I turned the handle and the door opened. And there, like a faithful dog, stood my brown suitcase. I stepped out into the corridor, there was no one to be seen, and I went towards the glass door that led outside. I was in a service lot of Brussels airport. A Sabena airplane thundered overhead and I knew I needed diplomatic assistance.

I took a taxi to the Swiss embassy. The embassy representative, a well-groomed man with big teeth that he bared in a smile at the end of every sentence, took care of me. It was hardly the end of the world, he reassured me, nor the end of my career. He gave me money to tide me over for a few days until the next flight left for Kigali and booked me a cheap hotel room. First thing Monday morning, he would brief my colleagues in Kigali. The man was very friendly and gave me tips on the local tourist attractions, but I was in no mood to go to see the Atomium or the Royal Museums of Fine Arts.

The bruises on my upper arms healed quickly, but the impression the woman had made on my soul ached for a long time. I was twenty-four years old, and I had read the *Négritude* writers, Césaire and Senghor and the rest of them. My bible was Haley's *Roots*, a book about the author's search for his ancestors, who had been captured in Gambia and shipped to North America as slaves. I had identified with the suffering of these captives, with their enslavement, with the thousand and one varieties of subjugation they had endured. These books showed me why you have to stand up for your beliefs from the very beginning and not wait for a convenient time to muster your moral courage. You need to engage it *immediately,* the very minute injustice is committed. Such acts of individual cowardice have made much of the world the pigsty it is. I believed this with every fiber of my being, but what good were ideals like these if the weak didn't want to be helped and refused the hand I offered them?

I spent the next week in my hotel room, agonizing over my future, leaving the room only to grab a quick meal in the corner restaurant. I still remember how I ran a bath on that first night to wash the shame from my body. I might as well leave these Africans in their own shit, and find someone who would appreciate my help. In Eastern Europe at that time, empires were collapsing like houses of cards. And why? Because the people were in revolt. Because they refused to keep silent. Those who don't rise up against injustice deserve what they get. That was my conviction, though I had to keep reminding myself of it, because the contemptuous clicking echoed in my head. The very first tart who came along had destroyed my ideals. What would it have cost her to make just a token gesture of appreciation? As soon as she saw someone weaker, she took the side of the powerful, of the oppressors. Because of her, I was stuck in a hostile city, in a neighborhood filled with grimy, dilapidated, run-down houses, in a lousy hotel room with a lime-streaked bathtub that was too short. I consoled myself by thinking that she couldn't possibly be a real African. She had probably been adopted by some interior decorators who wanted a chocolate-brown baby to complete their décor. It wasn't her fault she lacked social awareness; she denied her origins like every pariah turned parvenu. As soon as she allowed them to call

14

her a Negress, she forfeited every last shred of self-esteem. As I pulled out the bath plug, I saw her face before me, her unfortunately beautiful face, and in my mind I cursed her, calling her a Negress, at first under my breath, then more and more distinctly until finally I repeated the word out loud: *Negress, Negress, Negress.*

David repeats the offensive word like an incantation. He bends forward over the table before leaning back in his chair. In the wan and fading light, he seems a pale, colorless, gray figure and it's not hard to picture him shivering in the bathtub, alone and resentful.

I was saved by the World Cup, which Italy hosted that year, by the Indomitable Lions of Cameroon, to be exact. They beat Argentina in the opening match and moved to the top of their group. Just before my flight, they beat Colombia in the round of sixteen. I watched a lot of matches in my Brussels hotel room that week, but I wasn't as excited about any of them as I was about Cameroon playing England in the quarterfinals. The Africans led for most of the game, but lost in extra time because of a ridiculous penalty kick. I wanted to jump out the window. Once again the white men left the field victorious and all that was left for the eternal have-nots was the honor of being proud losers. But my disappointment was my salvation, since it proved my sympathies were still entirely with the right side, that is, with the underdogs. I decided to put the airport incident behind me. Instead of blaming the entire dark continent for one woman's despicable behavior, I'd give the Africans another chance.

If I'd been smart enough, I'd have learned my lesson and questioned my ideals and my reasons for wanting to devote myself to this work. But I was stupid. I was blind. I only saw what I wanted to see, and more than anything else, I had the childish desire to dedicate my life to a cause greater than myself.

A year before my departure, the winds of global politics had blown a few squalls my way. I joined the demonstrations, carried banners and shouted slogans, but the protests fizzled out after only a few weeks and the mildew of the established order spread over the country again. I'd had enough of Switzerland. I was fed up with its shopkeeper mentality and infamous ability to forget. Life was too precious for me to settle, as most of my friends had, for crawling into some hole, letting my hair grow long and wasting my time printing revolutionary rags in some stable turned squat. But it was also too precious for me to join the other side and demand my share of the pie as an ordinary office worker fighting for the biggest possible slice. I didn't want to be cannon fodder in the capitalist trenches. If I was going to sacrifice myself, it had to be for something worthwhile, and to find that, I had to leave. My country didn't need me, but down there, in Africa, even the tiniest portion of my modest knowledge was a fortune, and I wanted to share it.

And so I continued my interrupted journey and arrived one evening in Kigali. The first thing I noticed was the smell of wood fires and that darkness. We walked across the airfield and entered the badly lit airport. I was a bit nervous when I got to immigration, worried that the Belgians might have informed their colleagues in Kigali.

But everything went smoothly. My suitcase came out after just a few minutes and it wasn't long before I spotted a man in the Arrivals hall holding a sign with my name. As I went up to him, it struck me that he was too old for such long hair, which he had tied back in a ponytail, too old for the coral necklace he wore, too old and too pudgy for his tight leather trousers.

He introduced himself as Missland and welcomed me to the

'crown colony' with a broad smirk. Then he drove me down a dark road towards Kigali. He didn't say a word or ask any questions. He seemed preoccupied with his own thoughts. The car was filled with the smell of his aftershave and the throat lozenges he constantly slipped from one side of his mouth to the other. After half an hour, he stopped in front of the Presbyterian hostel, where I was to stay for a few days until they cleared the last traces of my predecessor out of my regular accommodation. My ground-floor room was at the end of an open veranda. It was simply, almost monastically furnished, as you'd expect in a Christian hostel. There was a table, a chair, and a wardrobe. A neon light buzzed on the ceiling. That was it. Missland handed me a few documents, a map of the city, and a note explaining how to get to the embassy, then left abruptly.

The woman who ran the hostel offered me a dinner of plantains, which I'd never tasted before, and a rather dry goat brochette that I washed down with strong tea. Beer and alcohol weren't permitted in the hostel, but the woman pointed out a bar at the end of the street, a good place to get a first taste of the local atmosphere. The gently sloping street was dark, but at the far end I could see a colorful glow that I assumed came from the tavern's sign. A dog barked, and the sound was so deep and angry I thought it would probably be better to put the visit off for another day and returned to my room.

It took me a long time to fall asleep. I was agitated and felt like my mind was still hovering somewhere over the Sahara. When I did finally doze off, the generator behind the house, which kicked on and off every few minutes, tore me from leaden dreams of smirking ducks' heads.

★

I was determined to forget the incident in Brussels, but the wound remained, and the life that awaited me in Kigali was hardly going to distract me from thinking about it. I'd envisioned a great adventure and expected to have to contend every day with the most abject human misery, but in fact my work involved updating address lists, typing project proposals, ordering stationery and fresh ink pads, even stuffing envelopes with invitations to the annual Development Day reception. During the day, I hardly noticed I was now two degrees south of the equator. The former embassy building, which housed the agency's cooperation office, resembled a vivarium, a cube with artificially reproduced native habitat. The heavy curtains muted the tropical sun and I often had the feeling I was sitting in my grandmother's parlor. Until her death, she had lived in the Bernese Oberland in the shadow of a mountain ridge and saw the sun less than five months of the year. It was strangely quiet, and everyone who entered the cooperation office instinctively lowered their voices, as if they were in a church or a doctor's waiting room.

Only once in those first few days did I dare call out a question to little Paul in his office at the far end of the hallway, but he didn't answer. Instead his face appeared in the doorway, flushed with anger, and he let me know that he expected me to get off my lazy butt and come to his desk if I wanted to speak to him. If there should be an urgent matter, I could use the phone, but nothing was ever urgent, I soon learned.

It was Paul, the Deputy Director and second-in-command in Kigali, who initiated me into the convoluted administrative channels, into the mysterious labyrinth of correct operational procedures in this universe of white, blue and green copies. When he explained the proper tab settings for reports on possible field projects for the operational section, I held my breath, not because the topic was that thrilling, but simply in an effort to follow Paul's explanations.

The noise level in the cooperation office never rose above that of a Protestant funeral. Even the long-distance radio receiver the size of an oven out in the hall didn't dare do more than whisper. The distant voices of Swiss Radio International murmured softly, shorn of any unpleasant high or low notes by the long-wave transmission. A thick gray carpet, patterned with maroon Swiss crosses which shrank to the size of dots then dissolved into the carpet's pile, swallowed the slightest impertinent noise, the click of a pencil dropped on my Formica desktop, for example, or little Paul's sneezing, which he did at least fifty times a day. The Deputy Director couldn't tolerate air conditioning and often had a cold. Because he was such a considerate person, he sneezed with his mouth closed and his face buried in the crook of his arm. At exactly two o'clock in the afternoon, the radio broadcasts ended and for hours afterwards Paul's furtive sneezing was the only sign that I wasn't alone. At those times the embassy seemed like a chilled mausoleum in which all life had been frozen. When we could no longer hear the women's laughter from the main hall – a single drawn-out vowel between an *a* and an *o* which sounded almost resigned, as if the woman had accepted the hopeless comedy of the latest calamity appearing before her in the guise of visa-seekers who would be turned away ninety-eight percent of the time – I would stand up cautiously and tiptoe over to Paul's office, where I would see the dwarfish man bent over some papers, his effeminate spectacles on his nose, with the desk lamp drawn so close that he bumped it with the slightest movement. I'd wait until little Paul made some movement, until he pushed the spectacles back up the bridge of his nose or played with the golden crucifix that hung from his neck, or turned a page. Only then could I be certain that time hadn't stopped and, consoled, I returned to my chair and looked at the damp crescents that constantly formed under my arms but disappeared when I raised them.

After work ended at five, I had just one hour of daylight left to explore Kigali. I watched the activity on Avenue de la Paix or drank a banana soda at Le Palmier. There wasn't much else to do in the city. Kigali was a sleepy backwater, orderly, neat, and boring. The first Resident of the German colonial power, a man named Kandt, had founded it eighty years earlier, in the middle of nowhere, at the geographic center of the old kingdom, not far from the ford in the Nyabarango River, which the dukes of Mecklenburg and Götzen had crossed some decades before that, becoming the first white men to set foot in this land. The settlement lay at the intersection of four roads that ran from Uganda in the east to the Congo in the west, and from the lowlands in the south to the highlands in the north, which is why Kigali was soon the country's most important commercial center.

Merchants from India and the Arabian peninsula settled there and sold their wares. German, French, and Belgian companies opened branches; a regiment of Askari, black soldiers from the coast of the Indian Ocean, protected the European masters. For a few years, it looked like the settlement would blossom into a real city, the first in a country that until then only had villages scattered among the hills.

After the Germans lost World War I and the Belgians cashed in on their assets from the bankrupt colony, Kigali began to decline. The new masters were suspicious of all larger cities, which they considered dens of depravity and fertile ground for unrest. They divided and conquered, backing the old monarchy and the Mwami, or King, who lived far from Kigali and had seen his influence wane with the new city's expansion. The Belgians had their own capital, Astrida, now called Butare, and Kigali did not rebound until the revolution of 1961, which overthrew the monarchy and drove out the Belgians. The young republic needed a new capital, free of the old ruling cliques and their influence, and so it began to develop the eastern side of the central hill in the Nyarungenge District, paving one street after another and installing streetlamps. Since no land had been set aside for the poor, who streamed into the city from every direction, ramshackle settlements soon sprouted in the nearby swampland. The narrow valleys were cultivated with cassava, bananas, beans, and coffee. From the swamps they took clay to build their huts and papyrus for their roofs. Still, the country never had real slums. All in all, Kigali was a peaceful spot. Its streets were clean and shaded by rosewood trees, and it was safer than most European cities. But it was also dreadfully boring. There were no public cinemas, no theaters, no concerts. People here didn't seem to need any distractions. In fact, they preferred uneventful days, and the less that happened, the better.

Only Saturdays brought some variety. I would stroll through Kyovou, the diplomats' and ministry officials' quarter, and skirt the center of town, heading south all the way to the mosque. In the Muslim quarter I would buy a meat skewer at one of the stands and wash it down with beer, watching the commotion around the regional stadium. Sometimes I would climb one of the hills, then leave the paved road behind me and set out into the fields.

Crops grew in chaotic profusion, as they had in the Garden of Eden: banana trees beside dark green cassava and millet, or sorghum, as tall as a man, and avocado trees interspersed with coffee plants. I liked following the narrow footpaths that snaked through the plantings and joined the brick huts plastered with dung. A reed-like plant called *miatsi* with stems as thick as pencils bordered the courtyards. The path led through a grove of eucalyptus and pine trees with needles hanging from the branches like long eyelashes. Dark violet flowers covered the ground. I felt as if I were being watched by a thousand cats' eyes, and shapes would suddenly emerge from the trees, silent, timid, and furtive. I could gradually make out faces, then all at once children would surround me, half-naked boys in tattered trousers, girls in shirts stiff with dirt. They were hill people with skin dyed by the red earth, hesitant and shy, but at some unknown signal, they lost all fear and joyfully fell upon the white man, screaming *Umuzungu! Umuzungu!* They pulled at my trousers and crawled between my legs. The commotion drew more and more children. They flowed out of the fields by the dozens and suddenly I no longer saw children, but gnomes or mountain trolls, and it wasn't at all clear whether they were well-disposed towards me or ready to tear me limb from limb, which they could easily have done. These scamps smelled of a life lived between cow dung and sour milk, and it occurred to me that it wouldn't be so bad to be like these children, to have dark skin and frizzy hair, to know my name but not how to write it, and to know by heart the secret names of all the plants – *imhati, amatehe, bicatsi,* and *amatunda*. And then that sharp smell would no longer stick in my nose, since I would smell of it, too, of fields, of milk, of cattle.

My first weeks in Kigali fell at the end of the good old days, the last few months of peace, and, like all peaceful eras, were boring.

It took less than three months for things to turn completely upside down and for the horror behind the veil of normality to become visible. But the agency hadn't the slightest sense of the imminent catastrophe. At the most, they anticipated a bit of unrest that could hardly pose a threat to our projects. Our greatest concern was the steep drop in the price of coffee. The Americans had ended the international export agreement. During the Cold War, they kept prices high to stop the coffee growers from going over to the Communists, but once there were no more Communists, the Americans lost interest in propping up prices. In the March before my arrival, export cooperatives received ninety cents for a pound of Arabica. One month later, in April, it was at seventy cents. Up until October, the price seemed to rally somewhat, but then, at exactly the moment the rebels attacked, it collapsed completely. At the end of the year, the farmers were paid half of what they'd got in January, a ridiculous forty-seven cents, and little by little it all went to Hell – first the growers, then the roasters, and finally the exporters. And what was this country's economy based on? On 35,000 tons of coffee, and a few tea bushes.

The price did not recover, not in January, not in February, nor in March.

We were grateful for a miserable five-cent increase in April, glad that the price didn't fall any further and stabilized near fifty cents through the following year. The agency paid the coffee growers fifty million Swiss francs in price supports. But it didn't help. The government had no revenue. The money eventually ran out and, with it, their means of soothing all discontent. The officials began casting about for new sources of revenue. 'He who pays the piper calls the tune,' as they say, and as soon as the President stopped paying, the pipers all called their own tunes. We heard that farmers in Gishwati had torn up their coffee bushes to plant bananas. They could always sell banana beer and, more importantly, the taxes weren't as high as those on coffee.

Time was against us. Each day brought the catastrophe a bit closer, but for me things improved day by day.

I stayed in the Presbyterian hostel for more than two weeks, longer than originally planned. I heard they were waiting for a shipment of paint from Switzerland to arrive in Kigali, but I saw the delay as a test of my 'frustration tolerance,' a term often used by the agency and an essential trait for the successful development worker I was meant to become. *Accommodation* – that was the word Marianne, the agency's Director, always used, never *apartment*, let alone *house*. So I was expecting a dive somewhere on the edge of town or at best a studio in one of the run-down houses near the main market, Kigali's only bad neighborhood, where guys with bloodshot eyes and rotten teeth hung around on street corners. I prepared myself for another exercise in humility, a lesson that would purge the last traces of arrogance from my spoiled European heart. So when little Paul took me to Amsar House, my first thought was that he was playing a joke on me. It was the most enchanting place anyone in my family had ever lived, a white-washed, one-story house with four rooms and a veranda that opened out into the garden, although the word 'garden' doesn't do justice to the colorful sea of powder-puff plants, crown-of-thorns, and Spanish flag. Half of it was shaded by an Indian coral tree and a wall four meters high, topped with shards of glass, enclosed the property. And that wasn't all. In the driveway stood my official car, a Toyota Corolla, well-used and with a few small dents, but that didn't matter. Now I had a car. I was a bit ashamed of all these privileges. I didn't know what I'd done to earn them. But, as I later learned, Amsar House was no personal distinction. It would have been impossible for an international organization to find a modest house in Kigali. No one outside of certain circles would have dared sell a house to a European. Many had got rich supplying foreigners with cars, clothing, office furniture, and security systems; and it was always the same ones, the *abakonde,* the people from the north who had been in charge since the military putsch seventeen years earlier.

My reservations didn't last long. The agency knew how to mold a man to his role. Because I wanted to show myself worthy of the house and the car, I took my work more seriously. I became more self-confident and my tone more polite and firm. Now, when I came across negligence at work – if the mailroom had run out of stamps yet again, or if a package from the head office had arrived but not been delivered – and they tried to pacify me with the excuses I'd always accepted before, I demanded the problem be solved immediately. I also paid more attention to how I dressed. Every morning I put on a clean shirt and shaved carefully. Even though my work was just as tedious, I was now always conscious of my responsibility. I didn't recognize it in the work itself, but in my privileges. The position came with a house so that I could rest after work. I needed my own car so that I wouldn't be exhausted by having to travel by bus and taxi. All this proved just how important my position was.

To get an idea of our department's work, I had to visit the various projects, and so I accompanied little Paul *into the field,* as they called it. It's a small country, so the trips were short. It took just three hours to get to our forestry school on the lake. Wherever we went, the locals were respectful, not to say submissive. In the Nyamishaba Forestry Institute, the director reviewed the graduating class. Two dozen close-cropped students in blue smocks stood at attention, chins raised, next to their desks. When one was called upon, he took a half step to the side and rattled off a list of Latin names – *Podocarpus falcatus, Magnistipulata butayei, Macaranga neomildbraedania* – the holy trinity of trees cultivated for building material. Another boy explained the function of each in toolmaking or in carpentry. A third listed their advantages and disadvantages – susceptibility to worm infestation, limited growth, significant water reabsorption – all in phrases apparently learned by heart, offered up by the blue-gowned altar boys of silviculture, who intoned their forestry liturgy without understanding a single word. After their presentation, the class called out, *Muraho, monsieur l'administrateur, Muraho!* and I expected that they would at least sing the national anthem and raise the flag, but little Paul dragged me out to the schoolyard, which had a view of the whole of Lake Kivu.

Seagulls circled above us, disappeared in the white crests of the waves, and reappeared further out in screaming flocks over the fishing boats. It's their way of showing gratitude, little Paul answered me, as if he had read the unspoken question in my embarrassed expression. And they certainly have reason to be grateful. He suddenly put his finger conspiratorially to his lips and looked around to make sure no one was listening. Thirty thousand, he whispered, each of them costs us thirty thousand Swiss francs a year. What I had just seen were the front-line troops of development, because in this country war was constantly being waged over each and every tree. These soldiers are expensive, of course, he admitted, but we have no choice. Someone has to carry our message up into the hills. Should we just let the farmers cut down the few remaining trees and leave them to their bare, eroded ground? No, we can't do that. In the end, we want to make it to heaven and how can we manage that except through good deeds? Paul's comments smacked of self-justification and I didn't understand against whom or what the school needed to be defended until I later learned the extent of the crisis in which the Institute was mired. Each year two dozen foresters graduated with diplomas but no work, because there was hardly a single forest left in this country. No one wanted forests either, since the farmers would all rather grow plantains for their home-brewed beer. In the entire country there were only two large areas of forest left: the rainforest on the slopes of the Virungas, which had been spared because the gorillas that lived there brought in good money, and the Nyungwe, the country's last old-growth forest. This was our primary battle-ground, since the farmers couldn't wait to chop it down, burn the wood, and roast slaughtered chimpanzees on the pyre.

There are people who protect them from destruction, Paul said. There was one such development hero I should meet, one of our two-dozen experts who do the dirty work out in the field. We drove further south, where the landscape was hillier, and soon reached groves of clove and sausage trees. After a while, two tidy houses appeared between the trees. A red flag with a white cross fluttered cheerfully in the breeze above them. Two children greeted us, little blond angels on the edge of the wilderness, their bare feet filthy, but their souls untouched by any corrupting influence of civilization. Their father, who was called 'the General,' took care of a protective belt of pine and eucalyptus trees he had personally planted around the virgin forest. He herded a company of front-line troops from the Nyamishaba Forestry Institute before him, not letting them out of his sight for a minute because, while the Latin name for every type of weed had been drummed into their heads, no one had taught them how to work for even half an hour without supervision.

His wife tended the garden, grew vegetables and potatoes and raised chickens and rabbits, so that all they needed to purchase was rice, sugar, oil, and coffee. In her spare time, she schooled her children in one of the cabins set up as a classroom. She taught them reading, writing, and arithmetic, and told them about their native country, with its mountains and lakes that were pictured in cheap prints hung on the walls, but of which they had no memory. The children's mother tongue was just that – their mother's language. Their vocabulary, learned only from their parents, sounded strangely foreign, too adult, too serious, without any of the nonsense words that are learned from other children. They answered our questions tersely and precisely, using phrases like 'self-evidently' and 'development horizon,' and accompanied us out to a freshly cut clearing, where the General showed us a gap some heretics had slashed into the belt of pines so they could cut down six or seven of Nyungwe's primeval giants. One they had sawed down but hadn't been able to carry away in their hurry still lay there, and the children climbed on the trunk like big game hunters on a slain elephant. This tree was more than two hundred and fifty years old, the General said. It alone had held several hectoliters of water – the farmers had no idea what damage they were doing with their desecration of the forest. The forest functions as a reservoir; it absorbs water like a sponge, then releases it into the land in small doses. Without the Nyumgwe, they would drown like rats, because the rivers would flood their banks with every rainfall. But how can you explain such things to a farmer whose language only has one word for the past and the future and doesn't distinguish between what happened yesterday and what might happen tomorrow? They're only interested in what today brings, and if that's wood to burn, then it's a good day.

Night fell soon after and we fled into the cabin. We ate dinner in the small room. The boy said grace and we ate our soup in silence. In the dim light of a carbide lamp, I could see the forester's callused hands, their wrinkles engrained with dirt, the mother's much-darned shirt, and the deep furrows privation had carved in their faces. And I thought of Amsar House, my upholstered office chair, and my orderly eight-hour day. In that moment, I regretted being an office drone, a paper-pusher far removed from any true challenges, sheltered from actual problems and all that was real and difficult and required daily hard work instead of idealism and grand theories.

After dinner, the children said goodnight with a song, one sung by Napoleon's soldiers as they crossed the Berezina. They sang of the journey that resembles our life, the journey of a traveler in the night, of the inevitable sorrows, but also of the need for courage because in the morning the friendly sun will rise again. The children gave their parents a kiss on each cheek. We remained sitting for a while, and the woman served coffee so weak that even in the carbide lamp's dim light, we could see the spoon clearly through the thin brew. The General brought the conversation round to a man named Goldmann, who worked as a forestry engineer in the Butare arboretum, hinting that the man had got himself into difficulties. When we asked for details, he pressed his thumb to his lips as if it were the mouth of a bottle, rolled his eyes, and shook his head. Too tired to talk, he said no more. He was a man who could not sit for long without falling asleep. He soon withdrew and left little Paul and me alone with the woman. Dog-tired ourselves, we listened as she described her daily life, haltingly at first, since she so rarely spoke with anyone and was out of practice. Yet each word released another as if the sentences were dragging each other from silence. We listened to her long past midnight and learned of her battle with snails as big as fists that devoured her vegetables, of the miserable quality of the supplies she bought in the food cooperative, of the farmers' dissatisfaction with the low coffee prices, and so on. Although our heads were buzzing with exhaustion, we remained sitting, feeling almost duty-bound. In any case, it would have seemed selfish to insist on our sleep.

The General's allusion to Goldmann's difficulties worried little Paul, so on the way home we made a short detour through Butare, the Belgians' former capital. Before noon the next day we found the forestry engineer in his boarding house on the outskirts of the city. He lay there unconscious, with an enormous blood-soaked bandage around his head. On the floor next to his bed was an empty bottle of Johnny Walker and the acrid stench that filled the darkened room indicated that no one was taking care of this man, who must have been lying in his own filth for several days. The old Twa who ran the pension and watched us mistrustfully with deep-set eyes under bushy eyebrows flatly refused even to touch the wounded *umuzungu*. This didn't offend little Paul. He explained that the Twa were excellent potters and cunning hunters, although this woman had probably never touched a bow and arrow or a potter's wheel in her life. His implication was that some native skills were not compatible with civilized practices like nursing the sick.

That's how he was, little Paul. He loved the country without reservation. There he generously excused what he would have denounced at home. He didn't have a drop of the cynicism that infects so many after years of fruitless drudgery in international service. Despite his chronic sniffles, he enjoyed a perpetually cheerful disposition, largely thanks to the carrot sticks his wife Ines cleaned and packed for him in bags from the pharmacy every morning. He nibbled on these vegetables the entire way to Butare and boasted of the excellent state of his digestion, which he attributed to these carrots and was extremely unusual among the whites. The endless plantains, rice, and beer made the bowels lethargic and caused chronic constipation, but no one dared eat salad or unpeeled fruit for fear that their constipation would turn into its opposite. Given the state of the local toilets, the latter was decidedly the worse of the two possibilities.

We peeled off the injured forestry engineer's dirty clothes, cleaned him up, and unwound the bandage until a gaping wound was visible over his right ear. Little Paul disinfected it with a bit of whiskey and applied fresh gauze. Once we had lifted Goldmann back onto his bed, we walked to the infirmary, where we arranged a bed for him as well as transport on a stretcher. The doctor cleared a room for our man by sending home early a woman who had recently given birth and moving a dying old man into a corner of the hall. We were satisfied.

Goldmann was taken care of for the time being, and since it was already past noon and we didn't intend to leave for Kigali until the next day, we took a room in the Ibis, a hotel on the main street that even under the Belgians had been considered the best in town. It had a restaurant frequented by all the whites and higher officials. In the cloakroom I noticed an unusual umbrella with a handle shaped like a duck's head. As I was hanging up my jacket, the carved drake sneered at me. Who do we have here, it seemed to mock, it's our musketeer who got himself reamed by the immigration officers. So he made it to Butare. Let's see what he gets up to here. I froze, staring into its dull green eyes, and little Paul had to call me three times before I woke from my trance. Paul said he wanted to lie down for a while before we went the arboretum to find out more about Goldmann's accident.

There was no one in the restaurant except for two Americans drinking beer and eating brochettes. The concierge was laconic and claimed to have no idea whose umbrella it was. I sat alone at a table near the entrance from where I could see the cloakroom and the umbrella. I had no plan how to react. I didn't have the slightest idea what I wanted from this woman, even if it turned out to be her umbrella. All I felt was my heart beating high in my throat as I dreamed up a thousand possible remarks, which I immediately rejected. I sat there, waiting for my moment of revenge. But little Paul appeared barely an hour later, before anyone had come, puffy-eyed and rumpled, but rested and ready to put the world to rights again. We set off on foot to the arboretum on a hill just outside town.

The accident had happened two days earlier, the supervisor explained, when Goldmann was taking his usual lunchtime nap in the shade of a *Eucalyptus ficifolia*. He came into the office, covered with blood, and said he was leaving for the afternoon. Then he got in his car and drove to the infirmary where they dressed his wound and released him. The supervisor had personally checked on Goldmann in his boarding house and offered to drive him to the hospital in Kigali. But Goldmann refused, saying it was just a cut, hardly worth talking about. He said he would be at work in the morning. The supervisor had seen right away that the cut was deep, but was just a scratch compared to the injury the branch had done to Goldmann's pride.

We could see what the supervisor was talking about when he led us out to lot 103. That's where the accursed *ficifolia* stood. The branch still lay where it had hit Goldmann. It was a good ten meters long, as thick as an elephant's foot, and rotten at the base, obviously attacked by some fungus. Goldmann had planned to prune the infected branches to save the rest of the tree. He must have leaned his ladder on the wrong part of the branch, that is, on the section he was going to saw off. This was too stupid and should never happen to a forestry engineer, at least not to one who was sober and had his wits about him. The supervisor made it clear that Goldmann had shown up at the arboretum tipsy that day and little Paul, dumbfounded, asked why no one had prevented him from doing dangerous work in such a state. They'd tried, the supervisor said meekly, but Goldmann wouldn't let them: first, because saving the tree couldn't wait and second, because Goldmann wouldn't let anyone near his favorite eucalyptus. The man then made a face as if Goldmann were not the victim of a forestry accident, but of an unhappy love affair. *Ficifolia* were decorative and at the sight of the deep red blossoms sprinkled like drops of blood on the ground, I remembered with horror that one of these trees stood in the garden of Amsar House.

Only on the way back did I fully appreciate the arboretum's beauty. The trees had been carefully planted in rows like the columns of an enormous cathedral covered with a vault of greenery. Next to trees from other continents there were indigenous species like the *Newtonia* from the Nyungwe cloud forests, some of them overgrown with amaranth, a vine that blooms only once every ten years, when it puts forth the white, feathery blossom they call *urubogo*. From a distance, the crowns of the trees looked as if they were covered with moss. For the natives, it was a sign of misfortune, since the amaranth in flower brings war, famine, and drought.

The omens were doubly fulfilled. The smaller of the two catastrophes was Goldmann's death. An embarrassed doctor informed us that the forestry engineer had died shortly after four o'clock. I still remember how little Paul stood speechless for a time, staring at the doctor like a fish on dry land gasping for air. They tried everything, the doctor explained and added in his own defense that the infirmary had very limited resources, as we could plainly see, and there was little they could do against sepsis and so on, the usual complaints. He had no qualms about asking us to put in a good word for him at the appropriate institutions in Kigali, or if that was not possible, could we at least provide him with written confirmation that his clinic was not responsible for Goldmann's death. Paul didn't answer. He just stood there paralyzed. He simply couldn't believe this country would dare kill one of our colleagues – not after everything that Goldmann and the entire agency had done for the people here.

They had taken Goldmann's corpse down to the cellar and undressed him, but strangely they had left his underpants on, as if they were too ashamed to uncover an *umuzungu*'s genitals. Goldmann's jaw was bound shut with a strip of linen and the wound over his right ear seemed to have grown bigger, a flap of skin hung from his head like a piece of torn cloth.

We stood in this unrefrigerated cellar, more of a hole in the ground, and agreed that we had to bring Goldmann's body to Kigali as soon as possible and ship it back to Switzerland. However, since darkness was about to fall, we put off the search for a means of transport until the next morning. In Goldmann's office in the arboretum's administration building, we packed up his few possessions – photographs, a compass, terrain maps, and a few standard books. We skipped dinner, drank two double whiskeys, and soon went up to our room.

Goldmann's death was terrible, but, to be honest, the greater catastrophe for me was that by the time we returned to the Ibis, the umbrella had disappeared. I don't believe in magic, I never have, but a shadow of the country's superstitiousness fell over me that afternoon. It suddenly seemed plausible that all these events were inextricably linked: the incident in Brussels, the duck's head, Goldmann's death. I didn't know how and I racked my brains over it. I was furious with myself for not having waited longer that afternoon or left a message. I spent half the night looking over Goldmann's notes and the rest of the night I tossed and turned in bed, restless and troubled by bad dreams.

The next morning it rained cats and dogs, a sudden, violent downpour right in the middle of the dry season. Little Paul and I scoured the town for a hearse, but all we could find was a pick-up truck covered with chicken droppings, hardly a suitable vehicle for one of the agency's engineers, even a stone-cold dead one. In the meantime, the infirmary had prepared Goldmann for the journey to Kigali. They had washed his body and put it in a coffin made from *Eucalyptus tereticornis*. I had read something about this fast-growing eucalyptus in Goldmann's notes. German missionaries had brought one of these trees to Lake Kivu and in 1912 they chopped down that same tree, the country's first eucalyptus. Its wood was reddish brown, hard, durable, and rotted very slowly, which made it a poor choice for housing the dead.

The country was overpopulated and the situation in Butare

province was especially dire. For every dead person there were three newborns, more mouths that had to be fed somehow. If the country's population continued to grow at the same rate, it would double in fifteen years. Already the demand for land could not be met. The hills were cultivated all the way to their summits. Even the dead were begrudged their graves. Since no one wanted the land to lie fallow, goats were allowed to graze in the graveyard. After ten years the graves were dug up and often enough a coffin of *tereticornis* would emerge, completely intact. Goldmann had explained to the appropriate authorities that they should use a softer wood, such as *Eucalyptus pellita* or *Eucalyptus rubida*. In his notes he complained bitterly about the bureaucrats who heard him out and agreed with him, but still did nothing. Little Paul and I also suffered from the authorities' stubbornness. The wood was as heavy as lead and, worse luck, the coffin was too long to fit in Paul's Toyota Tercel, which we had to use as a hearse since there were no other options. Paul was briefly angry that we could not shut the tailgate and had to drive the man's mortal remains to Kigali like an old credenza. Well, this is Africa, he finally said, and tied the door up with a bungee cord.

The sky had long since cleared but the midday rain had turned the road into a skating rink. Paul drove to Kigali carefully. The car's heavily weighted back end often fishtailed on the curves. But what worried me most were the people who accompanied us on our journey. The news that two *abazungu*, two white men, were driving a dead colleague to Kigali traveled faster than our car. An endless procession of people made its way along the roads in this country from the first light of dawn to the last ray of the setting sun, a procession of people on their way to market, carrying their goods in wheelbarrows, women returning home from the fields

36

with baskets filled to the brim, men taking some document or other to the nearest municipal offices on foot. Just after Rubona, this stream of people turned into a funeral procession for the dead engineer. Those we passed stood still for a moment and turned towards us. Women set down the loads they were carrying, took their children by the hand, and anyone who was wearing a hat, lifted it.

In the days following Goldmann's death, I was distracted by the necessary formalities. We had to inform his next of kin, just a sister. Health officials required a pathology report. Goldmann's estate had to be inventoried. But once we had loaded the corpse in its lead casket onto the Sunday Sabena flight, the old routine returned. The days passed, one indistinguishable from the next, just as they had before. I had too much time on my hands, far too much time for mulling over the duck's head umbrella. The country had given me a sign, but it spoke in riddles, and, despite my best efforts, I could make no sense of it. I knew just one thing: I had to find that woman. I hadn't drawn a single picture since I left school. I don't enjoy drawing and I have no talent. But I took up paper and pencil and sat at my table. Gradually an object appeared that, with a fair amount of good will, could be called a duck's head. Encouraged, I kept at it. I drew a pair of eyes with arching brows. I sketched in the hair and the freckles and because I didn't know how to draw light-colored eyes, I wrote up a description: female, name unknown, mid-twenties, one meter seventy, well-groomed, proud. On the following Saturday, I left first thing for Butare, back to the Ibis. I strolled around town, showing my drawing to everyone I could find, but no one recognized the woman I was looking for.

Fine, I admit it was a terrible drawing. Even I could hardly see a resemblance. I might just as well have shown a picture of Daisy Duck. Most people assumed I was crazy, but only the children were honest enough to laugh at me openly.

Since I had no luck in Butare, I started searching in Kigali as well. I spent night after night in the clubs, even though I was convinced she was not one of those *femmes libres* in short skirts, with a bored expression, on the lookout for an *umuzungu* willing to marry her. But it became a sort of joke: I was looking where it was well-lit. Pretty soon my search became an excuse to hang around the nightclubs, where there were plenty of other women who were interested in me.

And that's where I met Missland again, the man with the ponytail who had picked me up at the airport. Now he wore silver jewelry and his small, beady eyes were constantly on the lookout for adventure. He resembled an old Indian, at least until he opened his mouth. Then he swore like a trooper. I let him drag me to bars I would never have gone near on my own. But the truth is, I didn't like him, especially when he started going on about God or the state of the world, about political relations, or some conspiracy or other led by some secret society, which he believed surrounded him on all sides. His favorite topic was the quality of ass at Chez Lando, a club that provided a continual supply of fresh tail to Europeans. Missland assumed the right to sample the most appealing first. He had come five or six years earlier as a specialist for the agency, but in what capacity, I never learned. Nor did I ever find out if he had resigned or been thrown out. The latter was much more likely. If his name ever came up at the cooperation office, expressions became grim and the subject was immediately changed.

Missland was married, for the third time, to a woman from Kigali. He saw marriage as a form of development aid and felt it would be unjust to limit his assistance to only one woman. In any case, this didn't keep him from maintaining a harem on the side, which often caused violent scenes. They're only after my money, he would occasionally sigh, but I console myself with the thought that all the *abazungu* are treated the same. Or do you think that they're polite to you and the other blokes in the agency because they think you're such great chaps?

His debauchery cast a bad light on all the foreigners, but especially on the Swiss. We were here to make a mark through our work: bean-cultivation projects, credit cooperatives, brickworks. When the time came for development workers to be transferred to new postings, nothing but their projects would remain. Only Missland seemed to want to make his own mark, to devote his life, his desires, and his passion to this country and its people, to father children, and make women unhappy. He didn't hold back. He was ruthless towards himself and everyone else. But above all, he was immune to the unacknowledged shame that directed the agency's work. We felt responsible for the misery the white man had brought to this continent and we worked hard to atone for our sins.

Although I couldn't stand him, I spent more and more time with Missland. He introduced me to expat society, and Kigali was seething with expats. Aid organizations were crazy about this country. They were stepping on each other's toes and there was literally not one hill that didn't have a development project, not one municipality whose school had not been reformed. Women everywhere were attending classes in family planning, and mayors were being trained by development organizations. Poverty and underdevelopment set no limits on ideas: slaughterhouses, water collection points, grain storage, textile workshops, maternity wards, telephone wires, school toilets, training programs for young farmers, model cheese dairies, storage bins – there was nothing this country didn't need and the 248 aid organizations constantly trumped each other's new projects.

Missland invited me to his club, the Kigali Hash Harriers, of which he was president. We drove out to Shyorongi. From up there we could see the bends in the Nyabarango River. I was neatly dressed in a shirt, jacket, and long trousers, so I was taken aback as I watched the expats get out of their cars in the parking lot below us. Most of them were wearing shorts and a few of them were in tracksuits. It certainly didn't appear to be a formal occasion. People greeted each other like old friends and before I knew what was happening, a Belgian and two German women had dragged me into the bushes. It took me a while before I figured out what they were looking for – bits of paper from shredded files that were meant to mark the trail. Missland, as president, had organized a hash run in the fields. Arrows showed the way. Circles with crosses indicated dead ends. We passed through several settlements where the farmers watched us suspiciously, and when we came to the second circle with a cross, the two women became very upset, babbling about a punishment that would be waiting for us.

Our group was indeed the last one back to base, where Missland and the other Hash Harriers stood jeering at us. They took up some chant and didn't stop until Missland had hung toilet seats around each of our necks. We stood in this pillory as the president passed the sentence. It was always the same punishment. The losers had to down a large bottle of Primus beer in one go. The Belgian had no problem doing this, but the two women couldn't even drink half. When they gave up, Missland grabbed their bottles and poured the rest of the beer down their underpants. The club members struck up a song about the two pisspots, and when it was my turn, I took a deep breath and gave it my all. Surprisingly, I downed the entire bottle. But it wasn't good enough. Because I was a virgin, as they said, a newcomer to hashing, Missland opened a new bottle and baptized me as a new member. We spent the rest of the afternoon drinking beer, cracking obscene jokes, and trading the latest expat gossip.

Word of my new social circle reached the cooperation office and they were not pleased. They were suspicious of other development organizations in general, and especially the private ones. The agency claimed seniority. After all, we'd been in the country for almost thirty years and had the best relations with local officials. They guarded this privilege jealously. Missland and his friends were not suitable companions for an agency employee, little Paul informed me. It was bad for morale and even worse for one's reputation. Still, I had to do something in my free time and Paul had nothing comparable to offer. He didn't indulge in any pastimes. He did his work and at the end of the day he left the office for home, for his wife Ines and young son, and his mineral collection, of course.

I was fascinated by Missland's lewd stories with their mix of rumor and fact, and by his mania for discovering ulterior motives, if not outright conspiracies, and for drawing connections between events that had nothing whatsoever to do with each other. His way of thinking was utterly different from that of the other specialists and development workers. He didn't care about the results, it was the process that interested him, the side roads and detours that could lead one astray. He had a weakness for moral corruption, particularly his own, and he didn't resist any temptation.

On weekends we drove to Lake Kivu or organized outings and safaris in the Akagera National Park. Uncouth as he was, Missland still seemed to be the only one who was really *here*, who let himself get dangerously close to this country but without giving in to that mixture of professional zeal and childish confidence that the others indulged in, even little Paul.

So why are you here, my friend, you and your famous agency? We were sitting together in Akagera one Sunday, eating roasted antelope in front of the bungalows. In the marshes we had seen black-winged stilts, common snipes and black-crowned cranes. We had paddled out to the island in Lake Ihema to see the residence of the old King of the Mubaris, where Stanley had spent ten desperate days in March 1877 on his unsuccessful search for the source of the Nile. Why are there more than two hundred different organizations working in this country? Why isn't there a single hill without a development project? Why this incredible urge to shove money up the President's ass? What do you think? If human welfare is truly these selfless do-gooders' deepest concern, why don't they pack their things and go to the Congo, to Katanga? I was there, and I can tell you – it's Hell. Children are dying right in the streets. Some die of diarrhea, some of malaria, and some from nothing more than a common cold. There's death at every street crossing, illness in every corner, depravity and despair in every face, but there is not one development worker to be seen. All they've got is a bunch of nuns, way past their prime, who get a thrill out of washing the feet of lepers and the dying. Why don't they just pack up their suitcases and go where the real misery is, instead of treading on each other's toes here? I'll tell you why. No one, not even the greatest lover of mankind would trade paradise for Hell. And Missland was right. There were no mosquitoes here, no malaria. It was never too hot or too cold. It was the land of eternal springtime, as they said, the opposite of the Congo, Conrad's Heart of Darkness, which lay beyond Lake Kivu and which we could see on a clear day. It gave us the chills to see the moisture rise in a heavy cloud from the forests in the Congo basin. In some provinces the plague was still raging. There was talk of plantations in the Katanga where the white masters, dead since 1963, still lay in their beds. We had all read Conrad's novel, but the world he describes had nothing to do with this one. We didn't identify with its protagonists, Kurtz or Marlow, either, although we enjoyed our relatives' admiring looks when they learned how close we were to the jungle. In reality, however, we were farther removed from it than those who lived in Europe. In Nyungwe every bird was counted and every tree was charted, a half dozen international treaties protected it. Should a rogue farmer ever dare to cut down even a three-year-old pine, he and his family were the shame of the entire country. There was no malaria, except in Bugarama Province, only occasional yellow fever, and no schistosomiasis. Ebola was unknown. On our hill the air was dry and clean, and no one would want to trade this place with a damp, mosquito-infested swamp. That was Missland's explanation and it was a good, reassuring one. But for him, it was only a small part of the real reason we had sought out this particular country.

The most important reason we loved this country, according to Missland, was that there were no Negroes. The people looked like Negroes, with dark skin and frizzy hair, but they were actually African Prussians, punctual, orderly, and exquisitely polite. They never spat on the ground. They hated music and were terrible dancers. And above all, their state worked. They did whatever the *abagetsi,* the top dogs, told them to do, and they did their work conscientiously and without complaining.

Furthermore, we were here because we'd always been here, since the early 1960s. It was our land. It belonged to us, just as much as it did to the natives. We were a part of their history and they were a part of ours. When the agency was founded at the beginning of the 1960s, it had looked for a country that was similar to ours: small, mountainous, inhabited by taciturn, suspicious, hardworking farmers, and by elegant, long-horned cows. We jokingly called it our 'crown colony.' And those who worked in the head office – the Section Head, the Director of Operative Services, all of those who made the agency's political decisions – had spent their first years in Kigali. As young university graduates, they were outraged by Lumumba's assassination. The Congo Crisis politicized them. They wanted to build up this country, strengthen its democratic institutions, wrest the economy from the capitalists' claws and train the farmers, who made up ninety percent of the population, in modern agricultural techniques. They founded credit cooperatives to reduce reliance on foreign capital. They built brickworks so that the natives could use local clay and not have to import building material. New types of beans were cultivated and erosion was fought with forestry projects. They sent in forestry engineers, agriculturists, men and women who could help. The directors did not see themselves as administrators, but as entrepreneurs. We didn't administer, we created. We rolled up our sleeves and made things happen, and that's why we didn't trust the paper-pushers in the Federal Department of Foreign Affairs, of which the agency was a part. Diplomats and other hand-wringers were our natural enemies, but more than anything else, we hated politics. For us, it was the devil's strategy to keep the real aid from reaching the people who needed it. Politicians didn't do anything, they just talked, and in this country, there were no politicians. There was just the one party, the National Republican Movement for Democracy and Development. Each child was automatically enrolled at birth. There was no free press, no freedom of movement. It was a dictatorship, but with a benevolent, respectable, conscientious dictator. We just called him Hab, because his name was too long and impossible to pronounce. He was a real bloke, an *umugabo,* cunning like a fighter, but modest and self-sacrificing – he didn't exempt himself from the Saturday communal work required of every citizen. Hab had long been pardoned for overthrowing the first president seventeen years before, back when he was Major General, and having him killed along with a few dozen of his most loyal followers. The new president was a giant, fifty years old and as strong as an ox. His timid smile exposed a gap in his teeth. He was a war-horse with a child's face, who worked side by side with simple farmers digging ditches, laying pipes, and draining swamps. The development workers – those from private organizations, whether Christian or socialist, and those from the government-sponsored agencies from Belgium or Canada or from the sister program in the Rheinland-Pfalz – all admired this Major General who kept military expenditures low, fought corruption, and only indulged in two known weaknesses. He collected Chinese antiquities and he had a powerful wife who pulled all the strings behind the scenes – a Lady Macbeth, as she was known amongst the expats, always furthering her own interests and those of the *akazu*, the 'little house,' as her clan was called.

For us, of course, a dictatorship was out of the question, even if we firmly believed that democracy was a privilege of the urban elite. We'd visited schools, but most of the farmers here were illiterate and easily led. Free elections would only have brought chaos, violence, and misery, and before anyone could be allowed to take part in politics, they first had to have their consciousness raised. That, in turn, was only possible if their living conditions were improved. We were experts, and we knew that this wasn't the best of all worlds, but it wasn't the worst either. At the most it was the fourth or fifth worst, and that was enough for us.

But there was also another factor. We appreciated the advantages, the sense of order, the healthy climate, but at the same time we sometimes wished we felt closer to the primal mother, to our deep origins, which were pulsing nearby. We would have liked to sweat more, to look more often into the whites of men's eyes, to meet madness at daybreak. We had a great deal to do. We could have labored seven days a week and not run out of work. And yet, we were bored. We sat at the heart of the dark continent, but it wasn't hot enough for real metaphysical horror. We would have liked to commune a bit with prehistory, but none of us had the slightest idea where or how we might find it.

This country had sold itself for development aid, and that's why many of us felt disdain for these people. They hadn't remained savage. They didn't sweat. They didn't dance. They didn't boil up medicinal herbs or drink psychedelic brews. What we couldn't understand was mysterious simply because we didn't speak their language. Learning it didn't seem worth the trouble. We didn't believe their language held any secrets or the key to anything hidden behind this country's mask. No, the natives were nice, pleasant folk: punctual, obedient, uneducated, simple, suspicious, frugal. They couldn't dance and didn't care for loud celebrations. When they drank, they did it in the privacy of their own homes. What could they possibly have to say? Their arguments were over inheritance and access to land. There were no secrets here, no mystery.

Missland claimed that these people had another, hidden face, an ugly, violent one they didn't show to anyone else. This was certainly true for him, since he moved in the lowest levels of society. He drank, whored, lent money and came into contact with elements that remained hidden from the rest of us ordinary aid workers. The petty criminals, bootleggers, whores, and black-market moneychangers formed the same underbelly you find throughout the world. Criminality forced these people into the shadows, not tradition or secret rituals or any hidden plan.

The people we interacted with were honest, very few of them placed much importance on money, and there was hardly any corruption. What could they have spent money on if they had it? A nice house in Kyovou and a modest car with a strong engine, that was the extent of the luxury allowed to the wealthy. They sent their children to boarding schools in France or Belgium and brought them home as soon as their education was finished. They apparently couldn't be happy anywhere else. Anything beyond this would have sparked envy, and that was deadly in a country where people lived on top of each other, where you couldn't make a move without being seen. Envy poisoned the pleasures of wealth. It was simply no fun to drive around in a luxury car. No one did it, not the ministers nor the businessmen, not even Hab. He drove an Opel and wore simple blue cotton suits.

Modesty was a social requirement and international donors loved these people for it. Hardly any other country received as much aid. Donors fell over each other to help this poor mountain country. We Swiss recognized ourselves in their frugality and love of order. Protestant down to his underwear (a shade of light blue since white would have been too showy), little Paul had an almost frightening ability to adapt to his environment. When he spoke with anyone from the Belgian embassy, after just a few sentences, his French took on their flat, nasal accent as convincingly as if he had spent years in Brussels. Once we toured a sawmill and after a few minutes little Paul was talking with the workers, who had never left their hill and probably never would, as if he had grown up with them. He joked with them and talked shop about planks and saw blades. He all but joined them for a beer after work. He offered everyone he met the little Paul they preferred. The locals did it, too. But the question remained – a question neither Paul nor Marianne, and certainly none of the other directors could answer – did the people here really change?

Nevertheless, people began saying the country was sinking into chaos. That was nonsense. There was no chaos. A few dead bodies in the street do not mean there's no order, not by a long shot.

All right, I admit there were more than a few dead bodies, but the only time chaos ever reigned in Kigali was when the Pope visited. It almost cost me my life and marked the end of the good old days. The war broke out soon after and it seemed as if the Polish Pope's visit was the first shot of the cannon.

On the Saturday morning of the Pope's visit, Missland stood at my door at Amsar House, freshly shaved, in a cloud of Old Spice, his long hair plastered back as if he had just stepped out of the shower. You don't want to miss the Vicar of Jesus Christ, do you? he asked. But I thought of the official directive, signed by Marianne and posted on the refrigerator in the kitchen in the office. It ordered all employees to observe house arrest for seventy-two hours. We advise personnel to store enough drinking water and provisions to spend the weekend comfortably in their homes. God knows why, but pretty soon there I was, sitting in Missland's car. Even in Kyovou, an unbelievable tumult had already begun. Groups of pilgrims moved along the streets and further away we could hear the dull roar of masses crowding towards the stadium. We made good progress, but when we reached Place de la Constitution, the flow of people on foot stopped. Missland put the car in low gear and we made our way through the crowd. They stood arm to arm and ear to ear. They hung from lampposts by the dozen, nuns next to half-naked drunks, government officials from the capital in suits and ties next to peasants from the northernmost provinces. They came from beyond the borders, from the forests of the Congo Basin and the Ugandan plains. They had crossed the mountains on foot and rowed across the lake, climbed down from the heights of the volcano and left behind their chrysanthemum fields. They came up from the south, where the hillsides were covered with potato plants. Carpenters came, as did lumbermen and blacksmiths, the only artisans left to their own devices by the aid organizations. They were a stubborn lot, rejecting any innovation because they enjoyed the prestige of their caste and were proud of their past, when they had supplied warriors and kings with spears. There were cowherds one would otherwise never lay eyes on and those the country spat out just for this one day: mothers with a child clutching each of their fingers; brick makers who had left behind their burning ovens; beer brewers who, for the first time in their lives, had not prepared the sorghum. They all streamed towards the regional stadium, where Christ's vicar was meant to appear wearing his snow-white miter and his pallium. They all wanted to see him, even though none of them had been invited. Only the intellectual elite had been invited – the journalists, diplomats, and ministry bureaucrats. And yet the simple people flowed towards him like air rushing into a vacuum and I, sitting in Missland's Toyota Cruiser, stupefied by the noise, finally recognized this country's real wealth: its people.

All those who were normally spread out across the country were gathering on the hills of Kigali, just as the clouds mass along the mountainsides at home or the mountain finches gather by the millions to eat beechnuts – they meet in enormous flocks, filling the air with their cries and turning the forest floor white with droppings. Just as those birds are drawn by something far greater than their own consciousness, these people were being driven by a force they couldn't resist. No army on earth could have stopped this mass of people. No wall could have held back this tide of humanity that flowed from Place de la Constitution up towards Hotel Baobab. And in the middle of it all, there I was, me, David Hohl, and that wretch Missland, red-cheeked and grinning. The crowd pushed through the Muslim quarter, slow as molasses, passed boarded-up windows and the barricaded mosque, built by the Libyans. There was no church in the entire country larger than this mosque. The government did not want the Pope to be confronted with an Islamic house of worship, so, for just this one day, a road had been built that circumvented the mosque. But the mob couldn't have cared less. It followed the path of least resistance through the poor neighborhoods until it dead-ended in the sloping square in front of the stadium. Missland's car came to a halt as well. We were adrift in our little craft on a sea of bodies. The scent of Missland's aftershave blended with the smell of nervous sweat.

Row, row, row your boat, Missland sang, beating time with his hand on the steering wheel. He tried hard to mask his fear, but things had been out of control for a while. Boys climbed onto the hood and the roof, which bent so much under their weight that we had to lean out of the way. Missland turned up the music. Phil Collins was bleating 'Against All Odds', and I cursed myself for following this lunatic. A young man who had been standing next to my window for some time suddenly fell, like grass cut by a mower. In the second before the crowd flowed into the space, I lunged against my door with all my strength. Those standing near it were pushed back. Missland yelled and tried to hold me back by my sleeve, but I slipped through the gap my door had opened.

I almost passed out from the smell of fear and stress, and for what seemed like an eternity, I was pressed against the car as if in a giant vice. Then, somewhere on the east side of the square, about a quarter of a mile away, a bus driver must have decided to release his passengers after their two-day journey and, after a delay of a minute or two, the pressure of the forty or fifty extra people pressing against the stadium momentarily loosened the grip that held me. I was pushed to the left, where there would have been a bit of space if, at that very moment, on the opposite side of the square, the prior of Kabgayi's Catholic center, who had been patiently waiting on a platform for someone to forge a path for him and his nuns, had not lost his temper. He realized that although he and his group of nuns were expected inside the stadium, unlike the majority of those gathered in the square, no one was going to come to his assistance, none of the police officers or any of the helpers in yellow and white T-shirts busy maintaining order throughout the city. If he didn't want to miss the Pope, he would have to help himself, so he raised his center's orange banner in his right arm, blew his whistle three times and started to march. His group began to move, thirty white wimples danced like tiny icebergs in the endless sea of people. Like the rest of the throng in the center of the square, I had nowhere to go. Some footballers were pushing us from the right and the wall of the Islamic center blocked our retreat. We could only move forward, towards the stadium. The press of bodies grew stronger and we surged towards the stadium with increasing force. Luckily, I ended up in the middle of the main stream, where there was less pressure against slower-moving groups of people. Colliding forces created whirlpools and bodies were pushed into each other. My legs had not been under my control for some time. A dramatic, thrilling power had me in its thrall. I was a part of something enormous, and this living behemoth was as powerful as three hills, a breathing, panting, stamping organism whose tail must have lain some five kilometers south in Avenue de la Démocratie. I was part of its head, here in front of the stadium, the smaller of the two stadiums in Kigali, ridiculously small.

Things started moving so much faster that my legs, forced into a trot, could barely keep the pace. If I had fallen, or just stumbled, that would have been the end. The current pushed me directly towards the gate, above which hung a sign that read 'Stade Régional de Kigali'. Underneath it I saw a narrow gap, a passage barely as wide as two men, in front of which security had placed a barrier. I had to reach this barrier. I could distinctly hear the thought as it passed not only through my head, but through the ten thousand or more heads around me, and channeled the current in one direction. It was if the damned were streaming towards the last gap in the heavenly gates as they closed. I saw people being squeezed against the wall to the left and the right of the opening. The crowd had been terrifyingly quiet, but now it suddenly erupted into a deafening roar. Before then I never knew how desperately one could thirst for space, and after this experience I understood what it must be like for the farmers up in the hills, crowded into every inch of free space. Each of the twelve children every woman bore in her lifetime devoured not just milk, porridge, and bread, but land as well. For the first time, I experienced the law of physical displacement with my bones, ligaments, cartilage, the fact that two things can't occupy the same space at the same time. I suddenly had the crazy idea that everyone crowded together here would fall through that gate and right out of this world into a black hole to make space in the universe for those pushing from behind. And at the same moment I noticed ten or twelve police officers in green uniforms converging on the passageway and removing the barrier. I praised them until I realized that they were not creating extra room, but closing the door from the inside. I yelled and my breathless cry was amplified a thousandfold, as if I had a thousand throats or a thousand voices gathered in my throat. The monster bellowed and the faces near mine suddenly contorted with pain. These faces had remained impassive until this point, as if they were used to throngs like this one. But now their eyes bulged out of their sockets, spittle flowed from open mouths, noses and cheeks were compressed. Only their teeth were immobile. I could feel the bones pressing against my chest. I didn't know if they were others' bones or my own. Then another force took hold of me and pushed me towards the wall with unbelievable speed, as if I were part of a human battering ram being used to demolish the enclosure. Two or three seconds later, there was no longer anyone in front of me. I was in direct contact with the wall and being scraped against it. I tasted brick and mortar and blood, and just before I finally lost consciousness, the ground dropped away beneath my feet. I felt like a fish caught in a net being heaved up onto a trawler. For a moment I sailed on the cresting wave of this human tide. They were grabbing and tearing at me, pulling me in two directions at once – from below, from where I'd just emerged, and from above, where they were lifting me. Then I heard a crack, as if something had snapped under the strain. I thought it was my cartilage, a ligament, maybe an entire limb. Something filled my mouth and I tried to spit it out, but I couldn't get it off my tongue. Everything went black and that was the end, almost the end, anyway. A white shape emerged from the rising fog, like a disco queen from dry ice, but it wasn't a woman. It was an old man in a loose and strangely stiff robe that looked as if it had been carved from elephant ivory. He was hardly as big as my thumb but he spoke with a voice as loud as thunder. To his right appeared small black men with purple caps like glands, who raised their high, childlike voices in a song deriding a stranger who had not wanted to learn. They sang almost joyfully, enthralled by their own rhythm. On a signal from the figure in white, this dwarfish gospel choir immediately stopped singing. The figure started to make a speech, at least that's what it seemed to be, since the individual words were unintelligible. They sounded Slavic, possibly Polish, but it wasn't necessary to know the language to understand what the little man was saying. He ranted and raved, he scolded and stamped, he hissed like a teapot on the stove. And I, the target of this tirade, must have been the devil incarnate, since this figure was not speaking to any human being, but to Satan. Why else would he have held a crucifix out towards me? The little man disappeared and the choir stopped singing. I heard other, harder sounds, earthly noises, and when I opened my eyes, I saw that I lay in a large room lined with beds occupied by the elect. A soft whimpering, pained but not desperate, hovered above the invalids.

On one of the walls hung a comforting white flag with a red cross. Groups of men stood near some of the pallets, like clusters of trees in vast field. They stood with heads bowed and hands clasped in prayer. Occasionally a metallic clatter broke the silence, a moment later a procession of a half dozen Red Cross helpers appeared in the doorway. The first one pulled a soup cart along the rows, the second ladled out servings, and the third handed the bowls to the patients. The other three did the same thing, but their canister held weak tea with lemon. Many of the invalids were too weak to hold their spoons, but everyone was fed. When the kindly sisters reached my row, the woman in the bed next to mine, impatient with hunger, sat up so abruptly she almost fell out of bed, just as I almost fell out of mine, but for an entirely different reason.

The woman who was handing tea to the patients in my row was in her mid-twenties, her cheekbones freckled like a leopard's coat and her eyebrows arched like bass clefs. She smiled at the patients as she served them their tea. I don't know what happened to me, but I was overcome by the sense of falling into an abyss that you get as you fall asleep, but I actually did fall and ended up on the floor. The women all rushed over. The two serving the soup, who were stronger than the rest, lifted me back up onto my bed. And then, Hallelujah! Agathe handed me a cup of tea and our hands touched. But my senses were too groggy to understand. Maybe she only nodded, maybe she said something, but she moved on to the next bed.

Little Paul visited me that same day. He brought the new issue of *Jeune Afrique,* along with fruit cut into small pieces and packed into pharmacy bags. Missland had escaped the throng unscathed. You were damn lucky, Paul told me, eight people died in front of the stadium. To be honest, I was relieved when he told me that Marianne was in Kibuye and wouldn't be able to visit me in hospital. My blissful smile whenever Agathe passed my bed must have astonished him. Maybe he thought I'd gone crazy. In any case he left me after a quarter of an hour.

I had all the time in the world to admire Agathe. She had a second duty along with serving tea. She handed out clean pajamas. I have never seen more solicitude, a gentler smile, or more profound humility. She seemed to give herself completely to her work, changing bandages and comforting the injured.

When I was alone, I gave thanks. I couldn't say to whom, but I was happy to have found something I thought I had lost. And it felt like love, love for this gentle woman, for this country with its humble people, love for the opportunity to serve a worthy cause. I was as delighted as at the beginning of each school year, when new notebooks were handed out and we resolved to try harder, to write neatly within the lines, to do our homework. It wasn't the schoolwork itself we looked forward to, but the prospect of a new beginning. The clocks were reset to zero and the neatly kept notebooks were simply evidence for others of one's own transformation. On my sickbed, I no longer remembered how quickly I reverted to my usual carelessness. I forgot the ink spots, the loose pages, the missing homework. I only wanted to be here, in Kigali. I wanted to be as efficient as this woman, as self-sacrificing and guided by a mission. I wanted to be an aid worker, nothing else.

★

My injuries were not serious and I was released from the hospital sooner than I wanted. When I showed up at the embassy the following Monday, the Director informed me that my disregard of the official directive was inexcusable and I was to remain in Kigali only until the end of the month, when I would then be transferred to the head office.

I had always been afraid of this woman, afraid of her bulk, her bitter disposition, which stemmed from the pain caused by her bad hip. She walked with a crutch that creaked with every step like a rotten ship's mast. Because of the noise, she deposited this ancient implement from the local clinic in the umbrella stand every morning and left it there for the entire day. Without her crutch, the Director had to follow a set course to make her way around the first floor. From her office, at the rear of the building, with a view of the adjacent gardens, Marianne lurched to the filing cabinet with the middle drawer always left open so that she could support herself on it. From there she lunged for the planter shaped like a staircase that screened off my desk. She used this as her next crutch until she finally made it to the window seat that ran the entire length of the corridor. To extend her reach, she supported herself on her knuckles, the way apes do. She should have had her hip replaced long before, but I eventually realized why she continually postponed the operation. She would have had to return to Switzerland to have it done. Many of the agency's employees returned home only when it was absolutely unavoidable, because they were afraid they might be forced to admit that they had lost their homeland and now felt like visitors where they had once felt at home. Letters to old friends and weekly telephone calls weren't enough to sustain close relationships, and gradually they lost touch. Marianne was not married and since her parents had died, she no longer had any reason to visit the country of her birth. She gave up the Christmas vacations that were once a fixture of her calendar. She started neglecting family obligations, made excuses for a niece's wedding and missed an uncle's funeral. After a time her home country was simply a source of guilty feelings, a bad memory she avoided and repressed as well as she could. That's why she endured her lameness and the pain that increased with every month. But her illness, her physical and her spiritual illness, if you can call it that, made her one of the agency's most effective directors. She had nothing outside her work. Her life revolved completely around her projects. All she had for family were her co-workers in Kigali, but she avoided intimate friendships. We were all here temporarily, and close relationships got in the way. They always ended with painful separations.

Marianne didn't ask for an explanation as to why I had disregarded the official directive. She was not interested in me and when I asked for a second chance, she stared at me in surprise. Our mission is this country's development, not yours, she said. As far as she was concerned, I could run through the Akagera stark naked. She couldn't have cared less. The only ones she cared about were the people working in the projects, busting their asses to improve a few lives. And she cared about the locals, too, the ones who sat in front of their homes for three hundred days of the year wondering what they should do with their time. She didn't care what people did with their lives as long as they had a choice. I'd had a choice, and I had chosen to act against the agency.

I didn't contradict her, because I was afraid she was right. How could I be sure that I wasn't acting out of pride, serving my own egotistical needs, following my confused feelings? I didn't trust myself or my motives. Maybe I only wanted to stay in Kigali to be near Agathe.

I should have said something to convince Marianne of my change of heart, but all I could do over the next few days was to show up at the office on time, fulfill my duties reasonably well, avoid Missland, and hope Marianne would notice my transformation and reconsider the transfer.

Agathe was waiting for me on the pavement in front of the office when I came out like a beaten dog. I almost didn't recognize her. She no longer looked like the angel from the hospital. She had reverted to the woman in the airport, caustic and distant. I never really came to grips with her transformations over the subsequent years. There wasn't just one Agathe. There were at least half a dozen and when I thought I had a handle on one, she had already become someone else. I couldn't read her expression or gauge her tone of voice. I could see she was laughing, but her words sounded hard, and she often appeared sad when she told funny stories.

She wanted to see how her patient was doing and invited me to the Pakistani food stand at the large roundabout. We ordered doughnuts and soda and talked about all the things we missed. She missed her life in Brussels and her friends there. I felt a stab of jealousy, but didn't dare ask if there was a man there for whom she had any special feelings. She considered her stay in Kigali lost time and was anxious to return to Brussels as soon as possible.

She complained about her cousins, young men from up north, where her parents had originally come from. They sat around the house and would not let her be. Each of them was convinced that Agathe was going to marry him. But that was out of the question – she would never marry a Ndinliliyimana. Agathe hated her family name as much as she hated her mother tongue, Kinyara-wanda, a Bantu dialect that was nearly impossible for a foreigner to master and rich in peculiar expressions. *The neck is grief's lid. Pain does not kill, memory does. Where women are in charge, the cudgel rules. He who repays his enemy with a cow, loses his herd.* I liked these maxims, but Agathe grimaced. For her, it was a language of yokels, without poetry, made only to spread gossip and super-stition and to sell a cow now and then. And, of course, she added pointedly, to keep a few secrets from the *abazungu*.

I remember the traffic came to a complete standstill at the roundabout on that particular afternoon because an oxcart lost its load. Enormous bales of old clothes lay like giant beetles all over the road. Drivers swerved like maniacs to avoid them.

As a matter of fact, no one in the agency understood the lan-guage, not even the diplomats. Only a few members of religious orders who were in the country for decades learned a bit of it, and even if they eventually got used to the endless series of conson-ants, they never mastered the proper pitches that differentiated two words written the same way, like 'disgust' and 'hat'. Agathe wanted a different family name, a clear, simple one like Blanc or Dupuis, and she would certainly not pass up any opportunity to acquire a European name through marriage. If only her father weren't around. He wanted to marry her off to one of her insufferable cousins. If she were lucky, he might let her choose between a yokel who'd never been further than Kigali and some-one who was intelligent enough to read books, but looked like a toad, as long as he was part of the family. Agathe's father had insisted she spend her summer holidays in Kigali and now he wouldn't let her go back to Brussels. She could finish her studies here. She had gone to Butare to see the university. That's why she was in the Ibis Hotel. I didn't tell her about Goldmann or her umbrella. I didn't even mention that we'd been there. Butare was out of the question for her, since she knew what would happen if she agreed to go. So she hoped to get out of Kigali as quickly as possible – she pronounced it Kigari with a palatal *r*, the only trace of her mother tongue, which doesn't distinguish between *l* and *r*. She had worked hard to speak pure French, free of any accent, but she couldn't manage the soft articulations and that was the only thing that gave away her origins.

The oxcart driver at the roundabout tried to load the bales of clothing back onto the cart, but they were too heavy for the scrawny man and none of the drivers leaning on their horns were willing to get out and help.

I was stupid enough to ask Agathe if her father wanted her to be happy. He was certainly not a monster, she said, but he owed his career to family connections in the same prefecture as President Hab. If he were a man with the same capacities, but from the south, he would be stamping forms in some back office somewhere. Agathe was his only daughter, his only opportunity to shore up family relations, which was especially critical at the moment, since he was about to be named head of the ministry's Information Office. His boss, the Minister of Information, had previously prevented his nomination and promoted a man to whom he was related by marriage instead. However, the minister had just lost his post because of the speech he gave at the stadium during the Pope's visit. His speech had made waves that spread all the way to the international press. Holy Father, the minister began, you have spoken of AIDS and love that is fulfilled within the bonds of matrimony. But what shall I say to the married couple out there in the hills who have one child after another, each of them emaciated, hollow-eyed, condemned to die of hunger? What shall I tell them, Holy Father, when they ask me what they should do with their love? And what shall I tell the young man condemned to perennial idleness and unemployment who has no idea how to control his urges but is forced by the laws of the Church and of society into an abstinence he can't possibly maintain? And my last question, Holy Father, is what I shall say to the four thousand AIDS orphans in Kigali when they want to know why their parents died? How can I comfort them if I want to enter the Kingdom of Heaven and to do so must follow the Catholic Church's morality, which seems to me to perpetuate the white man's dominance?

That is how this man spoke and a glacial silence filled the stadium until the Pope once again declared his position: No sexual relations outside marriage. No birth control.

A brave man, one could say. No one was used to candor on these topics. Still, the only thing the minister accomplished was his own dismissal. The Church was powerful and the government simply waited until the *abazungu* forgot this episode of freely expressed opinion. Then the minister was axed. His successor was a history professor from Butare and a loyal follower of the President. More importantly, he was related to Agathe's mother. His brother was married to Agathe's mother's sister. The repulsive cousins were his nephews and Agathe's marriage to one of them would be the return gift for her father's promotion.

She said that she loved her father, but hated the country, the wheeling and dealing and the cronyism, which were the real reason it remained underdeveloped. Because of them even traffic couldn't flow properly and that's why half an army had to be called in for a simple accident. And in fact, at that point, personnel carriers had arrived on the scene and uniformed solders jumped down from the seats. Two of them grabbed the oxcart driver and beat him as they dragged him off the road. Four others led away the oxen and the rest piled the bales of clothing onto the army truck.

Of course, I was disappointed that Agathe was just a spoiled brat, the daughter of a privileged family, as I'd guessed at the airport. Still, I believed I had seen her deeper being in the woman who had nursed the injured in the hospital. This humble, self-sacrificing person had touched me, not the impertinent girl sitting across from me, sucking morosely on her straw. I tried to win her over to her own country, to persuade her that the well-educated had a duty to their homeland, and didn't mention that my lack of discipline had just cost me my position. Once again, I felt compelled to convince this woman of my sincerity and believed that if I did, I would lead her to do the right thing and stay here. But it all only made sense if I could keep my posting. Since I didn't think I could convince Marianne of my conversion, little Paul was the only one who could help me.

I visited little Paul on the next free Saturday. Ines, his wife, served tea and oatcakes. We sat in the room he kept for his rock collection. There were four massive cabinets. Paul's finds were stored in their deep drawers, each sample in a carefully labeled box. In all I have a ton and a half of stone, Paul pointed out proudly. He had to get special authorization, whenever he was transferred, for the agency to cover the cost of transporting his collection. They didn't approve of his passion. He sipped his tea politely and tittered, resembling a spinster secretly delighted at some misbehavior.

The tea was horrible, some kind of Chinese smoked tea that

smelled of bacon and probably cost a fortune. With the dry, un-sweetened oatcakes, it made a thoroughly unpleasant combination. It was like taking gulps of a charred stable. Nonetheless I ate and I drank, as little Paul leaned back in his chair, gazed at the ceiling, and recounted how difficult it was to find specimens of specific stones. Paul could not rest until he had a piece of each mineral for his collection. Some were easy to find, he said, all you had to do was bend down. Sandstone and metaquartzite were naturally close to the surface. But it was different with volcanic minerals, he said, before suddenly leaping out of his chair and opening one of the drawers. With the tips of his fingers, he lifted a box that held an unremarkable, yellowish, porous pebble. For this piece of volcanic tuff, he had to climb Mount Nyiragongo, he announced triumphantly. The rangers took him for a lunatic because he was not interested in the gorillas, but only had eyes for rocks. In the case of the tuff, it was easy to find, compared to the difficulty of finding gabbro. He was still missing this unique mixture of pyroxene and amphibole, although he had already labeled its box. He had looked for it in Kibungu, on the southern edge of the Akagera. He had hired three farm hands and had them dig up the area.

Paul's eyes shone as if he were speaking of a mistress who was all the more desirable for rejecting him. He wanted to search for gabbro in Bugarama at some point, but first he was concentrating on ore, even though it was a mineral that could be found without any geological knowledge. On his own, he would never reach the most interesting layers, they were buried too deep. He depended on the mines. He could get tin ore and amblygonite for just a few francs. The more specialized minerals, like tungsten and cassiterite, however, required skillful negotiating. He showed me tin gravel from Gatumba and a particularly nice piece of beryl. Earlier, it would have been ground for lenses, he said. The German word for spectacles, *Brille,* comes from 'beryl'.

All of sudden, Paul's tone of voice changed. He closed the drawer and sat down, apparently trying to find the right words, as if he were preparing a thought that was difficult to communicate, or as if he wanted to reveal a secret. He was, at the moment, working on a system that was comparable to astrology or the Chinese lunar calendar. He had discovered that each type of stone had its corresponding personality. Most of the workers in the agency correlated with orthogneiss. These are metamorphosed igneous rock with various characteristics melded into a stable whole. The individual elements are indissolubly fused together, and the people in the agency, like the stones, are resistant to pressure. They can withstand a great deal, but woe to those who crack. They burst with a sharp, clean fracture of their personality – Paul made a gesture with his hand as if he were splitting the head of an imaginary colleague. What wears them down is not the misery we see in the course of our work, but the sense of home-lessness. Everyone thought Goldmann was tough and reliable, completely devoted to his work. He probably thought so himself. But he was a gneiss and so unsuitable for international service. What the department needs are mylonitic schists. Their base materials are loose and unable to withstand external pressure. The foreign culture grinds them down completely. Their personality crumbles into microscopic pieces. Nothing holds their components together, their substance is unconsolidated and erodes. It may seem, little Paul said maliciously, as if such personalities adapt to the host culture. They wear the local dress, make common cause with the natives, and feel that they are communing with the world spirit. According to Paul's theory, these were all hopeless attempts to hold the remains of their personality together. However, if they survived this phase, they condensed into hard, durable, yet supple characters who no longer looked for a home in foreign lands. They no longer needed a homeland. They poured themselves into their work without reservation. For Paul, these mylonitic schists – elastic, indestructible, impervious – were the most reliable and efficient coworkers.

Maybe he was right. Maybe my personality had already crumbled, I didn't care. It was far more important that Paul speak with Marianne and convince her to rescind the transfer. Now you owe me one, my young friend, he said and finished his tea.

The last days in September, which they call the *kanama*, were a period of waiting. The dry season ended, the harvest was brought in, and the country awaited the rains that would bring life back to the land. Until then, everyone had too much time on their hands. We didn't know the clouds would bring more than downpours. The coming rain would wash away the old life once and for all. It would be as if the world we'd known had drowned. But things hadn't yet gone that far.

Agathe wanted to return to Brussels to finish her studies. I had very little time to convince her. Did I want to sleep with her? The idea terrified me. Did I want to prove to her that I was good, that my intentions were honorable, not stupid or naïve? Yes. Did I manage to do this at all? No. Am I ugly? No idea. Am I stupid? Very possibly. Are those the reasons I could never win her over? Probably. Is it possible that she wasn't interested in me because my father was a chemist, solidly middle-class, nothing special? That's what I told myself. Did I not try hard enough? Far from it!

Did I make a mistake? Absolutely not. Did I choose the wrong time to tell her I loved her? I certainly couldn't have chosen a worse one. And when did I realize this? Immediately. In fact, I realized it in advance, I mean before we went to Gisenyi.

All month long there had been talk of troop movements on the other side of the Ugandan border. These rumors were nothing new, but this time they were more urgent and more definite. The rebels, we heard, were gathering in great numbers on the far side of the Ruhuhuma swamps and had turned the town of Kabale into a military camp. What gave rise to the greatest worry was the fact that Hab was out of the country. He had flown to New York to discuss new loans with World Bank officials. I should have known how risky a trip up near the northern border would be, but I wasn't going to let any khaki-colored specter ruin my weekend with Agathe. It was my very last chance. She wanted to return on Sunday afternoon and I had all my hopes pinned on that weekend. We left on Saturday morning and planned on starting back for Kigali very early on Sunday, with the sunrise, so that she could catch the two o'clock flight that afternoon. But that wasn't meant to be. If I managed to seduce her, maybe she would postpone her trip or even cancel it altogether. But for that, I needed a weekend on Lake Kivu, a hotel room, a few drinks, a rowboat and a beautiful sunset. Gisenyi had it all.

What did she think? I can't exactly claim she was dying to go, but she agreed anyway, maybe only because she knew that afterwards she would finally be rid of me, and why turn down a trip someone else was paying for? Admittedly, she insisted that we register at the hotel under false names, which offended me, but I told myself that going incognito would add some necessary spice to our tryst. My only problem was coming up with a suitable name. I chose the names Mr and Ms Leslie Parker because I had recently read a short story by an author with that name in a *Reader's Digest* lying around Amsar House, about a raccoon named Rascal whose fate had reduced me to tears. The concierge in the Hotel Regina looked at me suspiciously and shook his head. I was afraid he was going to ask for identification but he was simply unable to spell the foreign names. So I filled the form in myself, with a trembling hand. For Agathe, it seemed the most normal thing in the world. When the bellboy offered to bring Ms Leslie Parker's bags up to her room, Agathe nodded casually. I thought of what Missland had told me once: *They have a hidden face they don't show to anyone. They lie as if they were telling the truth.* And I wondered if this was the case with Agathe.

The room was neat but rather cramped, so we soon went for a walk. I tried to impress her with my stories about our work, and because we had just completed our bean cultivation project, I told her everything about these legumes, about broad beans, fava beans, horse beans, cowpeas, black-eyed peas, kidney beans, tic beans, bell beans, field beans, and butter beans. I surprised her with the fact that beans are very delicate plants. I myself had been amazed the first time I heard it, since the hard, dried beans seem so tough and are not exactly easy on the digestion. It just goes to show that you shouldn't judge by first impressions. Besides, the local folk wisdom says you know a person by his beans.

She just said she hated beans. She had been traumatized by them every single day of her childhood and one of Europe's advantages was the absence of beans as daily fare. We were less than half way to Goma and I was already out of the game. I quickly assured her that I didn't care much for beans either, unless they were green beans served with bacon and sausage, but when you don't have bacon or sausage, then beans are an indispensable source of protein. On top of that, they ripened during both rainy seasons and so provided two harvests a year. She couldn't deny these advantages, even if her personal taste favored something else. I risked a sideways glance and she just repeated that beans didn't interest her. I decided to talk about the difficulties of growing avocados instead, about how they must be propagated through grafting, otherwise genetic deterioration will set in by the second generation. But she said avocadoes didn't interest her either. As a matter of fact, she had no interest in agriculture at all. I pointed out that her country depended on agriculture for survival, and having no interest in agriculture was the same as having no interest in her homeland. That's exactly it, she replied, she wasn't interested in her homeland. I burst out laughing and she laughed too.

Why did she hate her country, I wanted to know, and she answered that she didn't hate it, no, she didn't hate it at all. It just didn't interest her. Its people didn't interest her, its politics didn't interest her, and its problems didn't interest her.

But it's lovely, I replied, especially with the lake, the promenade, and the almost Mediterranean climate.

Yes, she agreed, it's lovely, but it's not for me. When I leave, Lake Kivu will be just as lovely as it was before. It doesn't need me for that. I found her reasoning solipsistic and for a moment I considered telling her, not because I wanted to disagree with her, but because I hoped she wouldn't know what solipsistic meant and I could explain it to her. I decided against it and asked instead what did interest her. But I shouldn't have, since her answer hit me like a slap in the face. Well, to be honest, it was a bit more complicated than that. I'm interested in boys, was her answer, but I couldn't read her tone of voice or pick up the slightest ambiguity.

Her answer was clear, serious, and unembarrassed. She might just as well have said she was interested in nineteenth-century art or Lega ceremonial masks. Boys. I certainly wasn't one of them. All I could picture were broad-shouldered, experienced daredevils, and I wasn't even close.

For some reason, the wound still wasn't deep enough and I didn't want her to think an answer like that could throw me. And what interests you about boys, I asked, knowing how idiotic it was. She just snickered. At that moment, I imagined a whole line of well-hung men by the lake and pictured Agathe studying one after the other, very closely, like insects. But I, unfortunately, wouldn't fit the bill and had no choice but to change the subject.

I suggested we rent a boat, but she didn't want to. I couldn't believe this, everyone likes boat rides. When I pressed her, she admitted that she didn't know how to swim. I didn't accept that as an excuse and a few minutes later we were sitting in a small dinghy. She sat in the stern, wearing a life-vest that was much too big for her. I rowed, drenched in sweat from the sun beating down on the nape of my neck, while she clung to the rail. After a quarter of an hour she convinced me that a boat trip was not necessary and not always enjoyable.

By now, the promise of spending a night in a hotel room with Agathe was fading, but since I didn't yet know that we would have to spend the night in my Toyota rather than in a double bed, I clung to the hope that a bit of alcohol could improve the chances of Agathe kissing a boy who didn't interest her in a country that didn't interest her.

But at that point something intervened which had already destroyed a few romances in Kivu and filled its lake with corpses, a story that brought death and destruction to the land each time it was recounted. The first chapter had long been whispered from ear to ear, but new exponents were now proclaiming the tale at the top of their voices.

There was a secret, a secret that had this country in its grip, or rather, it wasn't a secret, since everyone knew about it; it was a taboo, a taboo that bound them all. It had determined the beginning of the story and intruded on everyone's personal life. People weren't just people. They weren't just shoemakers, farmers, doctors, drivers, sons, mothers, daughters, or whatever. First and foremost, you were either one of the Longs or one of the Shorts. Expats avoided these local terms – they were forbidden words, associated with calamity, with murder, expulsion, revolution, and war. And we never asked anyone their *affiliation,* as we called it, because we didn't know what exactly these groups were, whether they were tribes, ethnicities, or castes. But Short or Long, they all spoke the same language and we didn't have a foolproof way of telling them apart. Of course, there were tall Longs of above average height, with relatively light skin and fine noses and the short Shorts, more thick-set, with darker skin, broader noses, and fuller lips. If there had been only these two phenotypes, it would have been easy. Unfortunately, however, there were also short Longs and tall Shorts; Longs who were tall and dark-skinned, and light-skinned Shorts with fine noses, dark-skinned Longs with full lips – every possible combination. Nine out of ten times it was not clear who was a Short and who a Long.

But only the Europeans had trouble distinguishing them. The Shorts knew at first glance who was one of them. So did the Longs. We had no idea how they could recognize each other, if there was an invisible mark on their foreheads or if they had a particular odor. We could only be sure when we checked their identity cards. On these cards, the categories that did not apply were crossed out, as if the officials not only wanted to show each citizen what he was, but also to what groups he definitely did not belong, and therefore what fate he could expect: whether he would be allowed to study, to work in a ministry, or to become an officer. All of these opportunities were open only to Shorts, and inaccessible to Longs. Since independence in 1962, Longs had been excluded from schools, politics, and the military. Only the lower rungs of society were open to them, where the Shorts left them in peace, as long as they kept quiet and didn't protest their fate. Naturally, we found this oppression of the Longs unjust, but we explained it away as a Pandora's box of a problem, and anyone who wanted to resolve it in the name of equality and brotherhood ran the risk of unleashing violence and bloodshed. Security was more important than justice; in any case it was the precondition for justice. As such, of course, it was necessary to our development work. Hab and his government kept order and peace and so we were satisfied with assurances that, in accordance with their constitution, no one was discriminated against because of his or her background. Longs made up only ten percent of the population and there were quotas that gave Longs access to higher education and the ministries. Theoretically, these quotas were respected. That there was not a single Long mayor or minister was simply an unfortunate coincidence, for which the Longs them-selves were partly responsible. Over the centuries, they had op-pressed the Shorts. All the kings had been Longs. The Longs had established the monarchy, and at the agency, we didn't like aristocrats. Even in a democracy, the Longs had oppressed the Short majority, who had, incidentally, come to this country before the Longs, as far as anyone knew, although no one really knew all that much because their history had never been written, but passed down orally from generation to generation. Just to make things more complicated, there were those who were Shorter than the Shorts, like the Pygmies, the Twa, of whom Paul was so fond, who were reputed to have been the very first inhabitants of this country. However, nowadays they had all but disappeared. You saw them less frequently than you did elephants. The only traces of these hunters were a few hills named after the animals, now wiped out, that they had once hunted.

No one knew when the Shorts had driven out the Shorter, probably before recorded history. In any case, the Shorts had long since flattened entire forests, chased away the Twa and their prey, multiplied throughout this fruitful land and separated themselves into clans. They called their King the Supreme Cultivator. He ruled on questions of life and death and collected taxes. When he died, his corpse was dried over a fire and he was given servants for his journey to the next world. A forest was planted over his grave. Only in the north did a few of the Shorts' kingdoms survive into modern times because at some point nomadic herders moved down from the north, from Lake Albert and Bahr el-Gazal, the Gazelle River, which drains into the White Nile. No one knew how they did it, but after a short time, the herders had established dominion over the cultivators. Gihanga was the first of these new rulers. Around the year 1000, he led his followers through Mubari and settled in Gasabo, on the western shore of Lake Mohazi. His emblems were a drum and the hammer Rwoga, and his dynasty lasted 900 years. One of his descendents, Mutara Semugushi, believed in history's eternal renewal and proclaimed that the repeating cycle would last for 800 reigns and just as many kings, whose names Mutara Semugushi listed. First came Mutara, followed by Kigeri and Mibambwe, then came Yuhi and Cyilima, again Kigeri and Mibambwe and finally another Yuhi. So ended the first cycle and another began. Each ruler had his particular duties. The Yuhis were Kings of Fire and Peace and they were forbidden to cross the Nyabarango River. Their reign represented immobility. On the other hand, conquest was expected of the Kigeris and the Mibambwes. They could move freely throughout the land. One of their most celebrated representatives, Kigeri Nyamuheshera, advanced as far as Lake Edward and reconquered Gisaka. Mutara and Cyilima were Kings of Herders. They were allowed to cross the Nyabarango, but only once. They were not allowed to return. Because of this decree, every subject knew if his children or grandchildren would live in a time of peace or war, and because they wanted to regulate societal relations as well as eras, the kings established the system of *ubuhake*. A Long would, for example, cede a few cows to a Short and receive labor in return, the Short cultivating the fields or transporting goods. Except for the King, each man was both master of one who was poorer and subject to a man who was more powerful. A web of interdependencies determined one's life, but the ties were loose enough that an impoverished Long could drop in status and become a Short and a Short who had grown wealthy could rise to become a Long.

The Belgians who took over the country after the First World War left the old order in place, but replaced the web with a wall. They distributed identity cards which established, unalterably, who was Long and who was Short. Whoever owned more than ten cows was a Long. That he was, in fact, a Short was not important. The new masters divided and ruled and the invisible membrane solidified.

Across the continent, as Africans began to liberate themselves from the colonizers the Shorts rebelled too. The Longs, to whom the Belgians had granted status but not power, were too weak to defend themselves against the revolutionary uprisings that soon inflamed every corner of the country.

Was it not commendable that the Bishop of Kabgayi gave the Shorts hope? He was a Swiss citizen who placed himself at the head of the democratic movement in February 1959, with a pastoral letter in which he preached racial equality and divine law that granted the same fundamental rights to all individuals and social groups. When King Mutara Rudahigwa died that same year, the leaderless Longs were too much at odds to take an effective stand against the revolution. The bishop celebrated the requiem mass but rumors soon spread that he himself had ordered the King's assassination. This was certainly a lie, but it did clarify the loyalties to which we Swiss would be bound for the next thirty years. King Mutara's successor, Kigeli V, was deposed in 1961 and the Swiss Confederation then appointed an advisor to the young republic; shortly thereafter, the newly founded development agency began its work.

There were excesses, of course. Many Longs were murdered and many more were forced to flee, but aren't these the necessary birth pangs of a republic? Were the European nations founded solely by peaceful means? Was it not understandable that the agency had, for the past thirty years, considered this particular problem solved, at least until development had reached a stage at which real democratization could begin? And things had not gone that badly; there had been peace for thirty years. But then the monster rose again and repressed history rose again in the guise of the expelled Longs, returning home from their Ugandan exile, and because the Shorts had never allowed them to cross the border freely, the Longs sent their sons armed with rifles.

They attacked the day Agathe and I were in Gisenyi. We weren't alone in the restaurant. German development workers from the Rhineland-Palatinate partnership were having a birthday party on the veranda. They wore paper party hats and red plastic noses, and sang suggestive songs. All I knew was that the gin fizzes we had ordered were having their effect and inhibitions were lessening with each swallow.

Unfortunately, Agathe started gushing about Brussels again, about looking forward to the pleasures she'd had to do without for months. Once again, in front of me I had the woman from the airport, interested only in filling her free time with as much excitement as possible. And, with her easy morals, she was flirting. Unless there was a miracle, she was sure to breeze through her exams, and so on, without a single word of sadness at having to say goodbye, not a hint of sentimentality. I doubt she wasted a single thought on the fact that we were parting the next day.

To her, I was just part of Kigali, that deadly dull backwater of middle-class officials and legions of development workers, whose worries about the trade deficit, the falling coffee prices, and structural adjustment regulations were written plainly on their faces.

The alcohol and her conversation had already demoralized me, when the Germans suddenly fell silent and I noticed one of them trying to tune into a certain frequency on his transistor radio. The BBC's six o'clock bell rang out ominously. There was no other sound but the sputtering of a motorboat making rounds on the lake.

I stood up to ask what was going on and one of them told me

to be quiet. Another whispered that the rebels had already overrun the border posts in Kagitumba, shot a border guard and chased the others away. The road from Ruhengeri to Kigali is closed, he added, and I wondered how I was going to break the news to Agathe. Indeed, at first she didn't understand a single word, but then she sprang up as if bitten by a tarantula, gathered up her things and ran towards the Hotel Regina. I had to pay the check, which can take a while at places on Lake Kivu, especially when you only have large bills and the waiter has to go into town to get change, which is how it was.

Agathe had thrown our bags into the trunk of the car and was sitting behind the wheel. She took off, driving like a maniac down the curving road to Ruhengeri. We could not get any further. The Germans hadn't been wrong. Government troops had set up road blocks and wouldn't let anyone through. We drove back the way we came as far as Mukamiira. There we left the paved road and followed a dirt road that ran along Lake Karago. Pelicans and herons flew by. The road twisted in tight curves and I would have liked to take the opportunity to see the waterfalls. But Agathe kept driving, always towards the south. Night soon fell, but we were lucky. The moon, in its last quarter, bathed the region in an opaque light. The road got worse. Agathe steered around potholes and occasionally we passed through a settlement, past an administrative building, and then the endless banana groves and tea plantations swallowed us up again. The bumpy ride and constant jolting wore me down. At some point I nodded off until another pothole banged my head against the window and rudely woke me. We drove on, deeper into the night, through the fields and the treeless landscape. We drove uphill and down, followed the Gitshye and the Muhembe, and left Kabaya and Gaseke behind. Agathe drove on and on. I had to ask three times before she stopped to let me pee. She kept the motor running. I felt like death warmed over, from the alcohol, the driving, and my disappointed hopes. When I wanted to stretch my legs a bit, she honked impatiently for me to get back in the car.

Once we got lost on a road that came to a dead end in a tiny settlement. The headlamps revealed the squalor of the hut – an animal shelter, really, not much more comfortable than a fox's den and less artfully built than a swallow's nest. Twice I again suggested that we wait until daybreak. Her silence left no doubt that she intended to keep driving as long as there was gas in the tank. Eventually the old mines of Katumba appeared on our left and right, and we continued on through the Nyawarongo Valley, a tributary of the Kagera. The narrow road zigzagged up to the top of a peak, where we stopped a moment just before dawn. We fell silent before the view of the thousand hills that stretched to the horizon under the soft moonlight. The entire western part of the country lay before us like a Daubigny or Chodowiecki aquatint, and suddenly I was grateful for this night. No matter what might happen to us, I would always remember this trip and it didn't matter that Agathe stood crying softly and berating me as she lost hope of making it back to Kigali in time.

We followed the road as it descended steeply towards Gitarama, past rocky slopes where the stony ground had long been denuded of any topsoil. People appeared with the sun. Women, children, and men emerged from the fields and I realized that this land had only seemed deserted last night. We had been surrounded by sleeping people throughout our journey.

Well, of course, Agathe did miss her flight and, to my mind, it was simple justice. She thought she'd just be stuck in Kigali for a week and I thought so too. But she never left her country again. She could have left any number of times over the following four years, but somehow she became infected by the bacillus, the hatred that finally poisoned and killed her, even though I didn't notice any change for a long time and she carried on for a while, at least a year, maybe longer, drifting as she had before. I've often wondered what would have happened if I hadn't insisted back then on our little getaway. She would have left for Brussels, no question. We would never have seen each other again. I wouldn't have spent one hundred days in Kigali and Agathe would probably still be alive.

We heard that the government troops had beaten back the attack that same night, but the BBC reported the next day that the rebel forces were still in Kabiro, sixty kilometers inside the border. Hot on their heels came the refugees – men, women, and children who wanted to return to the land of their ancestors after forty years of waiting in Uganda. No one in Kigali thought much of the government troops or had any confidence in them. True, they were supplied with French weapons, Panhard tanks, and Gazelle helicopters, but the army was too small – hardly more than fifty thousand troops – to give people a sense of security. Furthermore, the soldiers hadn't yet seen fighting up close. They were cadets, well fed and well kitted out, but lazy, nothing like the old kings' armies of legendary warriors who protected the land from slave traders for centuries. The 'cockroaches', as they called the rebels, had inherited that mantle. After the Longs' expulsion in the 1960s, they had joined the Ugandan rebels' most powerful forces and declared victory. They knew how to fight and that's why we remained frightened and suspicious when we heard reports that the government forces had cut off the rebels' supply lines from Uganda.

Hab had thousands of people arrested. Many Longs were pulled off the streets and thrown into prison without being told on what grounds, including two women who worked at the agency as receptionists. This, of course, was intolerable and little Paul and Marianne complained to the Minister of Justice and demanded that the prison conditions be reviewed. We visited the prisons and were outraged – twenty people in cells built for five, clogged toilets, contaminated drinking water – but no matter how sharply our formal complaints were worded, in informal conversations we let the officials know whom we held responsible for this state of affairs and whose side we were on.

Wasn't it understandable, after all, that Marianne's rage and little Paul's anger should be directed solely at the rebels, at the war the rebels had instigated and which now threatened their projects, the work of almost thirty years and three generations of development workers? Weren't the rebels the ones responsible for the disorder, the murders, for all the problems that were sweeping the country? You could understand, in theory, that they wanted to return to their homeland, but they should not have forgotten that they were on the losing side in the 1961 revolution. Should the Sudeten Germans have been allowed to return home or the three million expelled Silesians? What would have happened to Europe if everyone wanted to return to places their parents had happened to live for a time? In the interests of peace, this should not be allowed. The pig-headed rebels were the ones who didn't understand that an old injustice cannot be made right through a new one. Besides, it wasn't even their homeland, even though they claimed it was. In Uganda, Museveni, whom they had supported in his war against Obote, had dropped the Longs. That was the reason for their attack.

I never told anyone, but I liked the commotion, the mood in Kigali, the roadblocks, and the recruits with their crew cuts who marched through Kigali bare-chested in rows of two. I liked the Foreign Legionnaires France dispatched less than two weeks after the start of the war and the way they drove their jeeps around Kigali at breakneck speed, with the shadow of war darkening their determined faces. Well, who doesn't like them? Not the Legionnaires themselves, I mean, but the atmosphere they bring. After all, very few signs of the war reached us in Kigali. The skirmishes all took place far away, up in the north on the Ugandan border.

There were restrictions. In the early months it was not a good idea to stay out after eight o'clock at night – later it was expressly forbidden. The police were rude, especially the new recruits. People were picked up, beaten for no reason, robbed, and incarcerated. Not even embassy personnel were spared. One night, the soldiers shot someone from the Kenyan embassy, which particularly outraged little Paul. These people are barbarians, he said, we don't even know whose side they're on. One thing was clear: we could be targets, too. Marianne increased the security measures. Each house got a watchman and an extra telephone and we stuck large signs reading SWISS on the agency cars.

The country was becoming important. We were no longer stuck in some forgotten country somewhere in Africa. I was now working in one of the world's hot spots. We were sitting on a powder keg, exciting, unsettling. The city was ruled by rumors and had become dark and unrecognizable. It was as if in the preceding years we had only seen the backdrop and suddenly someone had turned the stage set 180 degrees. From then on we lived in the dark intestines, in bare scaffolding, on the real side, the true side. The side that was attractive, orderly, and well-supplied had been an illusion.

We understood the people as little as we had before. We often didn't know what drove them. In any case, the permanent smile had vanished, the country had taken off its mask. Kigali was mentioned every day in the international press. Articles from *The New York Times* and *The Times,* from *Le Monde* and the *Neue Zürcher Zeitung* were passed around and discussed. We pretended to be indignant over the journalists' mistakes and cursory reports. In truth, they simply confirmed our superiority. We knew better than these scribblers squatting in the newsrooms of Nairobi, Cape Town or, at best, Kampala. We'd seen precious few of them in Kigali.

One day, in the embassy, I took a call from a reporter from a Swiss newspaper who actually wanted to speak with Marianne. He wanted to know about the security situation and for some reason I told him she was out of the office, out in the field, but that I could answer his questions just as well. I told him the truth, I just used a few dramatic words to describe some meaningless incidents. A few days later, I read his article in the paper, which gave the impression that even in broad daylight, violence and bloodshed filled the streets. He described his source as a high official in the Swiss delegation and I simply hoped that it wouldn't occur to anyone that I was the person behind this nameless figure. But of course it all came out anyway. Someone in the head office complained that the cooperation office was being alarmist and wanted to know why the agency, which was, after all, known for its discretion, was spreading propaganda about atrocities. Marianne scolded me and little Paul wouldn't speak to me for a week. I acted repentant, but secretly thought that the article proved my importance, and besides, no one could deny that Kigali had become dangerous.

The calm days had gone, but so had boredom. I found the sense of danger energizing. I slept less, drank more coffee, and was generally nervous, but I'm not sure if that was because of the war or the thing with Agathe. She had called and said that she was going to stay in Kigali. Her father wanted her near him. In the north, the situation was precarious and relatives had come from her hometown of Ruhengeri. An uncle, his wife, and five cousins were now living with them in their house on Avenue de la Jeunesse. There hadn't been much room to begin with and her mother needed all the help she could get to keep house and take care of the guests. Agathe wasn't used to living with her family after enjoying her independence in Brussels. The month following the Pope's visit had already been torture. And now she had to stay for who knows how long in this backwater where a woman couldn't go to a bar by herself and even in a normal restaurant would be harassed by some guy in a uniform from who knows where. I thought this would give us a chance to get to know each other better. But Agathe saw it differently. She didn't want to see me, first, because she blamed me for getting her stuck in Kigali, and second, because she was afraid she'd get a reputation as a flirt who hung out at Chez Lando looking for Europeans. She didn't tell me this to my face, but it was clear. On top of that, our relationship couldn't be kept hidden, so she'd have had to introduce me to her family, and the idea of introducing me to her father gave her nightmares.

I gave her time. Her yearning for a foreigner, for someone who didn't belong to her clan, led her back to me. We met in secret. Instead of playing tennis at the sports club on Saturday afternoons, she came to see me in Amsar House and poured her heart out. I'm dying of boredom, she said. My uncle is an ignorant blockhead. He has bad breath and stinks up our house with his aftershave, but even that would be bearable if it weren't for the cousins. They stalk me, and gape at me, and ambush me. They're the worst kind of hicks, she groaned. None of them has read more than one book. For them Kigali is a major city, can you imagine? And her favorite brother, the only one in the family who meant something to her, was always busy. He was the leader of his party, the Republican Democratic Movement. Instead of taking Agathe out, which would have been her only chance to have fun without a chaperone, he went to meetings, wrote pamphlets, agitated and argued constantly with their father on the veranda over the future of the country, the new constitution, the rebels' goals and so on. Agathe found it all tedious.

I was surprised at how little she talked about the war. For her, the unrest was just something that got in the way of an interesting time. She didn't seem to care one way or the other about her country's fate, or only in so far as it influenced her own. I couldn't understand this, but at the same time her I found her political wantonness amusing. I would have given a great deal to have as much going on in my country as there was here, even though no one had any idea where it was all leading or what the future might bring. I did understand her brother, Felicien. I would surely have thrown myself into the commotion like he did. Yet at the same time I was, of course, happy that Agathe didn't get involved but came to cry on my shoulder instead. We exchanged a few kisses, but what she really wanted was a friend she could rely on, someone who would listen, a boy from the other world. And I was careful not to pressure Agathe, but to give her the feeling that I understood her. I knew what she wanted most: long chats and banalities.

A ghost lived in Amsar House. The only signs of its existence were the smell of bleach, crisply ironed shirts in the closet, full cases of beer, and neatly stacked newspapers. Sometimes on a Saturday, a tapping noise would wake me and when I got up, I might see the passing shadow of a small, wiry figure. The ghost seemed to have found secret passages leading invisibly from one room to the next. I rarely heard any footsteps, just the whisper of bare feet on the ground. But one Saturday morning, just after I'd sat down, still in my underwear and unshaven, in front of the television with a cup of coffee to watch *King Solomon's Mines,* which Missland had loaned me, the ghost suddenly stood right in front of me. It was an ageless person, and it took me a while to realize that it must be a woman. Without looking at me, she mumbled a greeting and cleared away the empty bottles and pistachio shells from the night before. First I asked her name. Erneste. Where she lived. Down in the swamps. Alone? With my husband. Children? Seven. Who watched them when she worked? She looked away and went back to cleaning. I told little Paul about her. She was part of Amsar House, he explained, and had been for quite a few years. Couldn't she come on another day, I'd rather be alone on Saturdays. He shook his head. She cleans other houses, but I should just ignore her and do whatever I pleased. And be polite and firm. No friendly chats. Make it clear who is master of the house.

I tried, but couldn't manage it. I wasn't used to this role. I got caught up in conversations that were too personal. I gradually learned that she came from the south. She was a Long, although not a typical one. She was stocky, dark, and so small that her feet barely reached the pedals on her bicycle, an old one-speed Indian bicycle with a padded plank instead of a baggage rack and a sign over the front light: *The more you hurry, the sooner you'll be with God*. She lived in Kigali illegally. As a young married couple, she and her husband had taken advantage of the confusion just after the military coup in 1973 and moved to the capital without an official permit. For seventeen years they'd lived with the fear of being sent back to their hill. Erneste's husband was the youngest of ten children. When his father died, all that was left for the young couple was a plot of land no bigger than a mattress, too small to support them. Her husband eked out a living with odd jobs until he got a position as attendant on the Kigali–Gitarama bus route. When the oldest children were big enough to shovel clay from the swamps for the brickworks, he remembered his role as head of the family, quit his job, and contented himself with managing the money his wife and children earned – in other words, pocketing as much as he could and going once a week to the woman who brewed millet beer in a back room and drinking until either the money or the beer ran out.

Otherwise he did nothing. He sat in front of his house all day and listened to the radio. He didn't even bother taking care of the little plot where Erneste grew cassava, bananas, and avocados – not enough to feed nine mouths. She had to buy food, which was expensive and brought shame on the entire family. They didn't own enough land to feed themselves and having to go to the market was proof of their poverty.

I felt sorry for them, but more than that, I had a large garden. I let her use a narrow strip, right up against the wall on the sunny side. At first she was irritated, but the following Saturday, she tore up the paving stones and planted a vegetable garden. I didn't tell anyone, nor did I ask permission. It didn't occur to me that anyone would object. Why should they? On the contrary, the Longs had won a great deal of sympathy within the agency. We were starting to realize that we had been supporting racists and we rushed to do something for the victims, and those were mostly the Longs. We speeded up a project to develop human rights, a topic we hadn't spent a single day on in the previous thirty years. And we desperately sought ways to maintain the necessary equidistance from the two parties. We looked for innocuous projects no one could oppose. We went to see the children of Gisagara, forty-six orphans who lived out in the open, on their own, half-naked. At least one of them died each week. Flies fed on the pus that oozed from the wounds of those still living. They'd lost their parents to AIDS. No one could say how this virus had spread all the way to the remote Kivu Province. We only knew that twenty percent of the people in Kigali were infected, and in some rural communities, entire generations perished. Because this epidemic was spread only through the direct exchange of bodily fluids, these people had to have another, private morality alongside the official sexual morality decreed by the Catholic Church. The development workers judged their hypocrisy harshly. It's not what the locals did, but the fact that they absolutely refused to talk about it. They remained stubbornly silent, would not use condoms, and seemed more prudish than girls in a church choir. I'm not the only one who found this surprising. I'd assumed that Africans were more comfortable with the 'natural' state than we Europeans were, but we weren't so different. They couldn't tell us how this virus had spread and those who were healthy decided the best medicine was to keep silent and isolate the sick until they died. Their orphans could fend for themselves.

We wanted to build an orphanage in Gisagara with a school and a dispensary. So Paul and I met the mayor for a dinner of tough chicken in the community's only eatery. It wasn't the first time we had been there. The man turned our proposal down flat. Before he would consider an orphanage, he needed a road, and to build a road, he needed a telephone. In his opinion, the hill of Gisagara deserved a road more than the orphans deserved a school. All the members of his community should benefit, not just the orphans. Otherwise he couldn't guarantee the children's safety, since the farmers would be jealous when they saw the beautiful new school and the dispensary. They would look at their own children, whom they could barely afford to send to school, and they'd look at the orphans, whose lives should be harder according to the law of nature.

We had no choice. For better or worse, the children were at the mercy of the farmers' good will. One day, we would leave and hand the institution over to the locals. If we wanted the children's lives to improve permanently, we needed the farmers' agreement.

That is why we sat there, in the community's only bar, sipping millet beer, while the mayor scooted back and forth on his chair and smoothed invisible wrinkles from his Donald Duck tie. His broad face wore an expression of permanent cheerfulness. He gnawed the cartilage from the chicken bones and blustered about his education at the technical school in Kigali. Like all of Rwanda's 840 mayors, he had been personally appointed to his office by the President. In theory, the local council held authority, but since most of the councilors had only gone to primary school, the mayor led the council like a bull with a nose ring. Each community was divided into ten sections, and these in turn were divided up into cells. The cells were not just administrative units, but were divisions of the political party. There were no independent structures and even the lowest-level leaders were controlled by the administration in Kigali. Each citizen knew his place and his superiors and followed orders that came directly from the capital.

Later, there would be a great deal written in the European newspapers about tribal violence and archaic brutality, but the truth is that the genocide was only possible because this country controlled the life of every single citizen and allotted him a specific place in society. No one could escape. Flying under the radar was impossible. Everyone had to play his part, no matter what role he was assigned. Everyone knew everything. No one could hide. Spies were at work everywhere and that is why the mayor knew all about me.

We were just fighting the 'battle of the basket' and, of course, losing once again. The waiter brought the check in the usual woven basket. In Paul's view, the mayor had invited us and so should pay the bill, but we couldn't simply tell him that to his face. He steadfastly ignored the little basket and told us his life story, that he was only temporarily the head of this backward community, only until the designated position for him in the ministerial bureaucracy in Kigali opened up. He explained his origins, those of his father, and his father's role in the revolution. He talked and talked and only once abruptly changed the topic when little Paul excused himself, leaving the mayor and me alone for a moment. He wanted to know if vegetable gardens were a tradition in my country. I didn't understand at first, until he maliciously hinted that he knew I allowed my staff to grow avocados, tomatoes, and cassava in my garden. He wanted to know if I would also let them keep goats or at least chickens, since everyone knew that a lack of protein was a major problem for those disgusting, scrawny creatures, those cockroaches, those *inyenzi,* our enemies' allies, underhanded assassins of the republic. I'd better watch out that *I* didn't end up growing vegetables for my cockroaches one day, because everyone knew how they good they were at scheming. All it takes is one slip, and they're the masters. Little Paul returned before I could ask the mayor how he knew all this. He stopped talking and was suddenly cheerful again. The battle of the basket continued. Paul was determined not to give in and, just this once, to play the game to the bitter end, so he began describing his rock collection, starting with the top compartment of the first cabinet. In that section, in the lower drawer on the right was a pyrite from Indonesia from his very first posting with the agency. Then he made his way, compartment by compartment, through his however many hundreds of samples. He didn't try to shorten his account of each stone's origin, its special characteristics, and technical uses, or to use language a non-specialist could understand. On the contrary, he savored the technical terms and after ten minutes I was so bored I expected the mayor to give in and pay the bill, just to be rid of him. I was right, but only in part. Instead of picking up the tab, the mayor just leaned back in his chair and rested his chin on his chest. After three breaths, a deep snoring filled the room.

That's how they won all their little basket duels and that's how they got their paved road. First, they weren't embarrassed to snore in front of strangers, and second, they had all the time in the world and just as much patience. We let the man sleep, paid, and drove back to Kigali. Paul fumed and said he'd never met a tougher mayor. He couldn't understand such pig-headedness. But he finally gave up. He realized the man would never change his mind. And so, in the end, I requested the construction of an extension from highway thirteen to the community of Gisagara.

It was granted even before the appointment of the purchasing cooperative's new Chairman, in whose honor a small celebration was planned at the central office. When Paul came to collect me at Amsar House, I'd forgotten all about the vegetable garden. I remembered it with a flash of horror only while I was putting on my tie and watching Paul as he stood on the veranda, staring at the beds. What's that, then, David? he asked. A vegetable patch, I answered, trying to sound as matter of fact as possible, but he looked at me blankly. Where did I find time for gardening, he wanted to know, and I had to explain who was growing the vegetables and that my wholehearted commitment to development in this country had resulted in doubling the calories available for a family of eight. And I reminded him of the victory gardens that our fathers and grandfathers cultivated to help our country get through the war. He only became more puzzled and I slowly realized just how bad an idea he thought it was. That's not on, my young friend, he bellowed, that is really not on. Things looked bad indeed, because whenever he called me 'my young friend,' a reprimand always followed. But for the moment he didn't say anything, he just told me to hurry.

In the car I tried to bridge the uncomfortable silence with excuses, saying that Erneste would give me a few vegetables now and then, but he slapped the steering wheel with his hand, then yanked it round, slammed on the brakes and stopped the car at the side of the road. He yelled at me, called me a stubborn mule and intolerably obstinate. Agency employees could not ignore the realities of this country, and one of the most important was that there were hierarchies. Erneste didn't just clean the expats' houses, she cleaned the houses of the officials who decided the fates of projects. And these people could make our lives very difficult if they learned that we were letting the household staff use our gardens to grow vegetables. If we let our own staff keep us on leashes, then the minister would lead us by the nose. I finally began to understand why the mayor insisted on getting his road. He took us for weaklings, philanthropists you could milk for whatever you wanted. My little vegetable garden cost the agency a road, a few hundred Swiss francs, money we might as well have fed to the pigs. There was exactly one car in Gisagara that could use this road. It belonged to the mayor.

But worse things were coming for little Paul and he suddenly had to get a hold of himself. A figure appeared in the rearview mirror, an *umuzungu* in a grass-green jacket, around fifty years old, bald with large spectacles and a narrow, lipless mouth. He was neither fat nor thin, but perhaps a bit bloated, like many whites in the tropics. The man clutched a battered leather briefcase under his arm and the way he shuffled up to the purchasing co-operative's headquarters made him look like a schoolteacher. When little Paul leapt out of the car and rushed up to him with open arms as if they hadn't seen each other for years, I realized he wasn't just some teacher. I had an idea who this man must be from all the allusions, whispers, and rumors, but I hadn't yet met him.

Some people called him Rasputin, others Cardinal Mazarin. In any case, he was the President's advisor and the most powerful European in the country. On top of that, he was one of us, a Swiss. From the first days of our work in the country, the agency had provided the President with an advisor. Jeannot counseled the President on all economic and financial matters, wrote his speeches, and developed strategies for dealing with the World Bank. All government documents passed across his desk. The agency paid him, but we had no influence over him. He wrote no reports and received no directives. He would have ignored them in any case. He rarely, if ever, came to the agency, yet we all knew how little he thought of our work. He knew everything about us, but we knew next to nothing about him. Sometimes we called him the Invisible Man, and he obviously cultivated an aura of mystery. He lived on Rue de l'Armée in the residence of the former ambassador, who had left Kigali a few years earlier. The only extravagance Jeannot allowed himself was the red paint on his old Mazda.

Paul introduced me to Jeannot. A sapling, he said, growing well but still uncut. Jeannot's lipless mouth did not move so much as a millimeter. He scrutinized me through his enormous spectacles, like a lizard, just one brief second, after which he seemed to have assessed and classified me. We don't want to keep the new Chairman waiting, he said, whereupon little Paul ran back to the car and I walked the last few steps with Jeannot. An administrator, then, he said to me, and I didn't know if it was a statement or a question. At that moment, two men came up to us, maybe businessmen, maybe officials, men in suits, at any rate. One of them was speaking to the other, who didn't seem to be listening, but stared at us instead. When we drew even with them, he elbowed his talking companion in the ribs, and the latter realized who they were passing. They greeted Jeannot as one. Jeannot just nodded.

Paul had parked the car in front of the purchasing cooperative building, had got out and we could see him waiting for us. But Jeannot stopped abruptly. I continued for two or three more steps before I realized he was no longer with me. I turned around and took a step back towards the President's advisor, who in turn set off, so that I had to hurry after him. I've heard you're interested in vegetable gardens? Very nice. I have a garden, too. Some plots in Kyovou must be contaminated and who knows what strange fruit will grow. So be on your guard, my friend, be on your guard.

We went to the inauguration of the new Chairman, the sixth in just a few years, each more incompetent than the last, but all the more loyal to the President. The purchasing cooperative was founded by one of the Belgian presidents in the 1950s. At the time, Europeans and Pakistanis dominated the retail market, but they cheated the farmers, paying them badly. The cooperative's mission, therefore, was to pay the farmers a decent price and to sell their products to consumers at a small markup. Soon after the development agency was established in Rwanda, it assumed responsibility for running the cooperative and over the years turned it into one of the country's most important business enterprises. We bought most of each year's coffee harvest and sold our products at the same price throughout the entire country. They cost the same in the capital as in the most remote corners of the land. We had our own school, and our newspaper was the most widely read in the country. And we had five hundred employees. But problems developed soon after Hab's *putsch*. The government began putting pressure on the executive directors and gained more and more influence over the cooperative. They put the Chief Financial Officer in prison, probably for political reasons, and replaced him with a more amenable CFO who knew nothing about inventory management and even less about balancing the books. Our specialists served only as advisors but we still supported the cooperative. We advanced funds when they couldn't meet the payroll, and when they needed a larger business center, we transferred seven million Swiss francs for a new administration building, a new library, a new cafeteria, and workshops.

Still, the situation did not improve. The new building was much too ambitious and the interest finally brought the already precarious financial situation to a crisis. The executive officers changed every year. No one kept an eye on the market. The competition had not been asleep and had developed better products they could offer at a lower price. And although we invested thirty million in the cooperative over the years, Marianne and Jeannot still used the inauguration of each new Chairman as an opportunity to wax eloquent about fruitful cooperation between our two countries.

I returned straight home after the celebration, took a machete and hoe from the shed and tore up Erneste's plants. I did what I had to do, without anger or hatred. I dug up the cassava, cut down the tomato plants, and turned it all under. I knew that I had finally become a proper development worker, one who understood all the circumstances and didn't give in to sentimentality. Maybe this garden did help support a family of eight, but it had almost prevented us from building an orphanage. When Erneste arrived with her basket the following Saturday, she retrieved what vegetables she could and I let her know that I expected the flowerbeds to be restored.

At some point during those days, when we had grown used to the situation but the war was still far away, I finally won Agathe over. For me the big shag began, my great era of copulation: necking in the shower, making out on the veranda, quick fucks on a Sunday morning, endless sex in the evenings, petting on the porch, French kissing on the couch. Agathe and I had the whole house to make love in. We wanted to try out each of the five rooms and the more than thirty pieces of furniture as settings, and we loved them all, especially the uncomfortable ones like the dresser with the sharp edges or the chairs with the prickly sisal seat covers. I loved the brief exchanges after the initial movements, the assurances that we weren't out to rub each other raw, rational bits of conversation that cropped up in the midst of ecstasy. They reassured me that Agathe was fully conscious, that despite every-thing her desire remained reasonable and considered, and that these short interchanges – 'You OK?' and 'Keep going' and 'But first smooth this wrinkle out of the rug, it's digging into me' and 'I'm probably going to get a cramp, but whatever' – were proof of our bodies' vulnerabilities and sensitivities. And they reminded me that we were connected, holding onto each other tightly, lost in the physicality that seemed to be a source of desire, but was, in fact, an obstacle to fulfilling it, a limit on the ecstasy for which our bodies were simply a means, not an end.

No matter how often we made love, or how nakedly we offered ourselves to each other, I couldn't entirely escape a feeling of shame. For Agathe, the sexual act didn't seem to have anything forbidden about it. At the most, it was a bit disreputable, since we weren't married. She made love like she ate, to fulfill a need. She was no more responsible for this need than for the need to eat. It was simply there and made itself heard, just as a baby cries so that someone will take care of it. What I found most shocking was that Agathe seemed to know this need inside out. She knew what she wanted and even my desire held no secrets for her. I was an open book that she could read or put aside. It was all up to her. My obscurest desires, my epiphanies of passion were obvious to her, as clear as day. This transparency unnerved me, since I had no idea what needs deep within me were screaming to be satisfied. I didn't even know if it would be better just to let them whimper. I worried that the more I fed these needs, the more they would demand, and maybe it would have been smarter in the long run to ignore them contemptuously and let them starve. But when I saw Agathe, with the silver sheen on her skin, her lips and her gums the color of veal, I wanted to run my tongue over them. When I kissed Agathe, I wanted to take her, and when I felt her breasts, her bottom, her neck, I wanted to screw her, to plant my cock inside her, wherever she would take it. And then, when I was behind her or lay under her, in whatever position my desire had brought me, then I no longer knew what more I could possibly want, but I knew that I still hadn't reached my goal. Agathe didn't put up any resistance, which doesn't mean that she let me do everything. If she didn't like a particular position, she didn't say no, but offered an alternative. It all seemed the same to her, a finger in her anus was no more depraved than a kiss on the lips. She believed that once we had transgressed the moral boundary of having sex outside of marriage, nothing we did would aggravate our sin.

I could not understand this. I had all sorts of thoughts that I only allowed myself to think in certain circumstances and in the end it was exactly this shame, this fear of being a pervert, that attracted me most. My own indignation excited me and I couldn't conceive of how it could possibly work without that sense of shame.

Sometimes I believed my cock and its erectile tissue weren't filled with blood, but with shame. I was sure I was a pig, a lecher, because I only wanted to screw if screwing felt depraved. Would I have craved Agathe's ass if her anus didn't seem to be a gate to blasphemy? Once, on a Saturday, while Erneste was cleaning the house, we drove my Toyota about a half mile down the road in back of the sports club and parked it behind a hedge. This was damned reckless and could have cost us our lives. There could have been a farmer behind any of the banana trees and all of Kigali would have known by the next day. But we did it anyway. The danger and the lack of space in the backseat excited me; we had to get our arms and legs in a certain position to get them out of the way. Agathe screamed and I held my hand over her mouth. When we were done, she cleaned herself up, straightened her clothing and didn't say a single word about the insanity her desire had driven her to.

As we were driving back, I looked at her in the rearview mirror, searching for a sign, a wink, a movement of her lips. I wanted her to be an accomplice in debauchery, but for her, the decision to do it in the car was simply a logistical necessity, just as you look for a second restaurant when all the tables are taken in the first. We wanted to shag. Amsar House was full. So we shagged in the car. And that was it.

I was disappointed and began to wonder if there was possibly some pleasure in the act itself, in the mingling of our secretions, the contact of my dick with the insides of her orifices. Without question, this contact was pleasurable, but I most definitely wasn't doing this because of mucous membranes. None of this got in our way, but I longed for the moments when I would be alone and could think about shagging, not about the act itself, but rather about Agathe – not about her as a person or as a woman, but as a child of this country. I was proud of myself and my dick. We had left the hick town we came from, we moved out and overcame all the obstacles of our origins and of cultural differences. No prejudice kept us back. We just followed our real vocation, the hunt for cunt. That is what nature had intended for us. I should have explored this mystery, but until this point I couldn't even look at Agathe's pudendum calmly.

I often lay on the sofa and tried to picture it, always without success, her vulva was a Bermuda triangle in which my thoughts disappeared without a trace. Of course, I had a particular idea of it, but I didn't trust it. I was afraid I was picturing a cunt other than Agathe's, one from the magazines that we had found in the rubbish when we were boys. So then I would reimagine Agathe, starting with her head and feeling my way downwards from her hair. I could picture her face and neck quite clearly, her freckled nipples and her sweetly rounded belly, but then I lost focus. My mind's eye grew foggy. I could still make out her belly button, different from any I had ever seen, a knobby little bump that stuck out because the midwife had tied it off with a piece of wood that Agathe now wore around her neck as a good luck charm and never took off. Then, as if in the distance, the gentle swelling covered with hair and, even less distinctly, the frizzy tuft that resembled a stubble field – and that was it. I didn't get any further. Every time, I resolved to take a closer look at her anatomy the next time.

But when we were together, I was much too caught up with petting, with wonder at her perfection, which only an artist could have created, because it was inconceivable that human cells, those formless globs, could have formed themselves into something of such grace and softness. She lay there, bathed in my amazement, revealing the perfection of her limbs, the bromine-colored hollows of her knees, the transition from the lighter shade of her palms to the darker backs of her hands, her toes, those cheerful little gnomes with shining red faces, and the blue-plum shade of her fingernails. I was completely caught up in these moments. I was so much in the present that I couldn't memorize even the smallest detail. All that remained was a not entirely pleasant feeling of transience, and the fear that all I had were these moments, these hours with Agathe on the sofa, the evenings on the veranda, and that everything I couldn't capture at the time, anything I couldn't internalize, would be lost, would fade into the memory of the experience.

Paul took the war personally. It felt to him as if the rebels had attacked not only him and the work he had done in the six years since he had arrived in Kigali, but also the agency's work over the past thirty years. He grew even thinner than he'd been before and even quieter. He resisted going out into the field, where the projects were beset by more and more difficulties. He spent entire days holed up in his office and when I occasionally looked in on him, I rarely found him at work, but sitting upright at his desk, and I was startled when he caught my eye with an injured and accusatory look as if I were the one responsible for the injustice he was suffering. He no longer spoke at meetings, he just sulked and made no suggestions as to what course of action the administration should take. Often Marianne sent me out of the room after a few minutes and through the door I could hear her cajoling him.

We were sure he would soon leave his posting, and when he returned home for two weeks with his family during the Christmas holiday, in order to rest and to ski, I was convinced he would not come back. But there he was for the new year, rested and tanned, or rather, with his face glowing bright red. He almost disappeared into his baggy shirts when he pulled his head down in the enormous collars, like a tortoise pulling its head into its shell. But something had changed within him. The sense of mute offense had turned to taciturn defiance, and gradually his decisiveness seemed to return. Once, when we were out in Kigali, a patrol of French paratroopers overtook us. When their jeep drew level with ours, Paul called out, *Vive la France! Vive la république,* and he yelled so loud and with such zeal that I jumped and passers-by turned around to look at us. Masked by their sunglasses, the paratroopers drove on without the slightest reaction and I didn't know which republic Paul had meant, the French one or the republic here. What was clear, however, was which side he had chosen, namely, the side of the President, the Major General. Little Paul sided with those previously in power, those whom the French had come to defend.

Paul met frequently with Jeannot, who remained faithful to his President. Jeannot asked the agency to issue a public declaration of solidarity with the President. Hab, after all, was the only one who could maintain security and stability. Marianne claimed it was too early to choose sides. Only Paul was in favor of a declaration and he felt betrayed when the request was refused. It was precisely now, he argued, in these unsettled, chaotic times, that you have to make your position clear. He visited the overcrowded prisons to check on the prisoners reluctantly and only when he couldn't avoid it. He wasn't at all convinced these people were innocent. How can I know what they did, he said, they can't be sitting here for no reason. And after all, there's a war on, isn't there, a war this country has been forced into. A state has the right, no, the *duty*, to defend itself, and special situations require special measures. He pointed out that the country had been at peace and just because criticizing the President had suddenly become the latest trend, he wanted to remind everyone that the President had not wanted this war. Hab gave the country some good years, Paul declared bitterly. And now, what's going to happen now? They're going to authorize new political parties? Brilliant. Have any of you taken a good look at this so-called opposition party? I don't believe that you or I, or anyone else, could continue our work at all successfully with those old fogeys in power.

Although the new constitution still hadn't been approved and parties were officially banned, all sorts of clubs had formed. Among all those who aspired to political careers, there must have been a few honest people, but many had dubious reputations at best. One of the leaders of the Liberal Party was a convicted murderer. He had killed his wife and was free only because the President had pardoned him. Lawsuits had been filed against him for embezzlement of public funds and he probably just wanted to use his political influence to get out of paying off his debts. Another party leader, one who had written a humanist pamphlet that accused the government of corruption, mismanagement, and incompetence, which was a topic of fervent discussion throughout the development community, disappeared one day. Most people assumed he had been assassinated until word spread that he was in Kenya, living off his business partner's money. And the others, those with spotless reputations, were people who felt neglected by the President and wanted to use political positions to get even after being passed over.

The World Bank had forced the government to devalue the currency by forty percent, Paul said, coffee brings in less than cow manure, a band of wild mercenaries is inciting a war, and instead of standing by their President like men, these rascals are intriguing and creating even more chaos. Democracy? That's a beautiful idea, but they're not concerned about democracy. They just want to get rich.

At that time, Paul began catching flies with his hand. He didn't swat them, but caught them with his bare hand, or rather, he tried to catch them. He always missed when I was present. He was simply too slow for the flies, but the fact that he would even try to catch them showed that his determination had returned, and more importantly, so had his patience, since his failure to catch them didn't disconcert him. He just kept trying. His anger faded. At some point in the first years of the war, he realized he couldn't resist reality, and by the time the new constitution came into effect the following June, Paul was back to his old self.

It wasn't Marianne who helped him regain his belief in his work, it was Jeannot. They ate lunch together in Le Palmier and the adviser talked to him, explaining why the country needed people like little Paul now more than ever. Jeannot himself would stay on, even if his work was being criticized more and more openly. He had led the negotiations with the World Bank, negotiated the terms of the structural adjustment program, and no one knew what he had wrested from the gentlemen in New York. The general population no longer thought much of our Rasputin, because every one suffered the effects of the shock treatment he had prescribed for the country. At head office they discussed his resignation. Some felt his closeness with the President was no longer an advantage. Yet Marianne and Paul managed to keep him on the payroll for another year. I never laid eyes on Jeannot again. He remained invisible. No one ever discovered the exact role Jeannot played, how much influence he had with Hab, or if he was responsible for the increased extremism in Hab's politics. In any case, he was against political parties created because of pressure from international donors. He was against the Longs and their influence. One thing is certain: he devoted a few of his best years and all his knowledge to keeping a dictator in power. And we paid his wages.

The people wanted democracy, and who in this country was better suited to teach them the rules of the game than the Swiss Agency for Development and Cooperation? Little Paul recalled that we were service providers, and it was not up to us to decide what a country needed. We should confine our fervor, our wild passions, our needs, and our hunger for battle to rational, orderly channels, and what opportunity could be better than showing them how to run a proper radio station and give the guard dogs of democracy some teeth?

We were burning to start when the Minister of Information came to speak with us. Ferdinand was a polyglot professor of history with a degree from the Sorbonne, better versed in his country's history than most. He was an *intiti*, someone who had studied in Europe, and not one of those blockheads who had never set foot outside Kigali and their ministry offices. But it wasn't his idea, it had come from higher up – from Hab. Early in the new year, he met with our ambassador. The government wanted support for its information services. It was indignant at the international media's manipulation of the facts. And we were too. Hab's government was being portrayed unfairly. After years of seeing him as the guarantor of law and security, he had suddenly sunk to the level of an ordinary dictator. Things weren't perfect, it's true, but the regime deserved better press.

In April, the eighteenth month of the war and the height of the rainy season, Ferdinand came to the cooperation office. Rain was pouring down in a solid curtain of water, as if someone in the heavens had flooded all the swimming pools. It was a small delegation: the Minister of Information, his head of radio broadcasting, three lower-ranking officials, all modest, reserved, discreet men, who spoke softly in cultivated French and wore suits, nothing extravagant. In fact, the suits were rather worn, baggy at the elbows, a few had even been repaired with patches. These men were not what you'd call dapper. But at the agency we weren't either. There were no boutiques in Kigali. My colleagues ordered their wardrobes from abroad and their trousers often didn't fit properly. Sending packages back to Europe took a long time and was expensive. So they wore the badly fitting clothes anyway.

The embassy was comfortable. The building could have been modeled on Scrooge McDuck's safe. It was a cube, sided with red steel panels that resembled crenellations. Very little sun shone into the sitting room on the first floor, yet we didn't turn on the lights. We sat in the gloom and could barely make out any change of expression on the dark faces at the other end of the table, but the voices we heard were soft, friendly and humble. Ferdinand was an extremely polite man. Modest and reserved, he chose his words with care and made no demands. He pointed out problems and at the same time outlined possible solutions. The members of the delegation emphasized their desire to do better and always struck the right note. They had the will and lacked only the means. We rarely denied them anything. If there was enough money in the budget, they got it. He was the minister, after all. Our two national radio systems had worked together a few years earlier. Young journalists from Kigali were sent to Switzerland with a stipend from the agency. This collaboration was to be resumed. The journalists meant well, but they lacked the proper education or professional training. What was more important than a free press?

That's why we flew a journalist in from Switzerland, a short man with thick hair, slanted eyes and the habit of buttoning his jacket's top button into the bottom buttonhole. We paid for his airfare and two weeks in the country's best hotel. We gave him an honorarium that the average worker in Rwanda couldn't even earn in four years. At the end of the two weeks, he wrote a report with suggestions on how to improve the broadcasts. Ferdinand and his people set to work immediately. The broadcasts became livelier. They played music and explained to their listeners that they would no longer simply read the government's declarations word for word, but would offer critical commentary. We were satisfied and believed them. In any case, we had no way of checking on them, since they broadcast in their incomprehensible Bantu dialect.

We only realized how well they had implemented our suggestions shortly after Ferdinand was replaced. It wasn't that Hab was unhappy with him, on the contrary. His people had just gone a bit too far when they announced that they had uncovered a plot hatched by the cockroaches against government leaders, against politicians, officials, businessmen, but above all against people from Bugesera.

Soon after that announcement, the farmers in the Bugesera

District rose up in self-defense, as they called it, and killed the alleged accomplices of the rebels. We learned this from an article in the French press that quoted an Italian nun who had lived in the area for twenty years and had apparently managed to learn this obscure dialect. She described the incendiary speeches broadcast by Ferdinand. Not long after the broadcasts, it seems, strangers arrived in the district and meetings were called during which officials from the central government told the local farmers that they had uncovered a cockroach conspiracy. Apparently the Longs planned to kill the Shorts and to restore the monarchy. The farmers swarmed out of the meeting to 'clean out the bush' as they put it. They grabbed men, women, and children from their homes and murdered them on the spot. They set the houses on fire, stole the livestock, and moved on to the next hill, where they continued their 'work.' They threw the corpses in the latrine pits.

Little Paul shook his head as he read me the article, but not so much because of the horror, and certainly not because of our bad judgment in teaching Ferdinand and his people how to spread propaganda effectively. He was angry that the nun was foolish enough to give her whole name. And he was proven right. Three days later the nun was dead. She was shot with two bullets, one in the mouth she couldn't keep shut, the other in her reckless heart.

Ferdinand had rather overdone it and, with a heavy heart, Hab sent him back to his professorship in Butare. Yet this clever man had apparently learned enough about running a successful and popular radio station to set up his own. He gave the announcers free reign to express their views about the cockroaches and their allies. I occasionally listened to the station during those hundred days and the few scraps of vocabulary I'd learned from Agathe were enough for me to understand the calls to murder, the lists of names read over the air, the calls not to give up before all the cockroaches were exterminated, before all the graves were filled. They had learned the lesson. The broadcasts were entertaining. They played music, performed short sketches in which two shrewd farmers discussed the stupidity of the *inkotanyi*, as they called the members of the rebel army. Fine, it wasn't our intention to teach the *génocidaires* how to do their work, and it was certainly not our fault if they used the radio as a murder weapon, but somehow I could never shake the feeling that I was observing one of the agency's more successful projects.

At some point, I believe it was in the second rainy season after the war had begun, Agathe cut her hair; to be more precise, she shaved her head. But I didn't attach much importance to this. Of course I missed her former artful hairstyles, the thin braids she had woven into elaborate frets and labyrinths, but I understood when she explained that this was not a time to spend hours at the hairdresser's. She still spoke more or less as before and hadn't yet taken up the singsong she adopted later. Her French was without accent, perhaps a touch nasal as one might imagine a Belgian accent, and when she talked about the war, still far in the north at the time, she sounded worried, not angry. She condemned the rebels, not so much for their goals as for the consequences of their actions.

She was not alone. God knows we all agreed. The rebels lacked manners and good will and we had no desire to discuss their claims as long as they were uncouth and anything but peaceable. We were upstanding people. Our virtuousness and our irreproachable morals bound us to those who were under attack, to those who had never wanted anything more than food and clothing for their families. We came to this country with a mission, in pursuit of an idea, but these rogues, who looked to us like the caricatures we saw in the papers – thin as a rail, with huge hats on their tiny heads and even larger shoes at the end of their long legs – these brutes had no ideas or morality. They had lost two countries, the one that drove them out thirty years before, and the one in which they became fighters who were no longer tolerated. For us, none of that justified their actions.

It was not enough to demand a homeland. It was not enough to demand reparation for past injustice. It was not enough to want to restore their fathers' honor. Not only did these demands not justify their actions, they were criminal if they jeopardized work in the fields, education in the schools, and peace throughout country. We were Europeans, we knew who had lost the war, and we knew that they had to accept defeat, even if their expulsion had been against the law. Reparation would have required a new crime, a new war, and the point was to break the eternal cycle of revenge and retribution, to swallow the bitter pill for the greater good, not for the sake of themselves and their lives as soldiers without a country. Their lives were already botched. All the future held for them was death in a foreign country. There would be no consolation prize and they simply had to accept it. If they needed grounds for hope, then they could believe in a better future for their brothers' children, those who still lived in this country and for whose benefit we struggled every day, with greater and greater effort, in longer and longer conferences and meetings.

Each day brought new difficulties and we had to explain ourselves to all sides. The head office wanted reports. The ministers in Kigali wanted professions of loyalty, which we could only give if there was sufficient mutual trust, and that meant that we would have to criticize them for their own good. If, under the pressure of attack, they allowed the social order they had so arduously built up to collapse, if they imprisoned people without trial, if they sent mobs out into the hills, then our government would quickly lose all sympathy for them. We told them very clearly why we liked them. It was not because of their poverty, their dark skin, because poor people and dark-skinned people could be found in great numbers in many places. What bound us to them was essentially their integrity. We admired them for virtues that are considered secondary, but that for us were of primary importance: orderliness, neatness, and honesty. Most important of all, however, was that they were hardworking.

We expected absolute devotion to the mission from them, and that's why we demanded that they give the prisoners fresh air, nourishing food, enough water and exercise, and, above all, that they treat the prisoners properly. When we did have to criticize them, when we weren't satisfied, we let the officials know that our unhappiness was not a sign of disloyalty. On the contrary, it was a sign of our love, just as a child is scolded because he is loved, because we know the rules that govern the world and destroy those who don't follow them. It was not acceptable to round people up at night, kill them, and burn down their houses, or to incite murder over the radio. This was just not done, whether or not they had good reason. Even if this were their custom and always had been, even if murder were part of their culture – it had to stop. Television and cameras had been invented and, though the international press had shown little interest when this was a small, peaceful, quiet country in the heart of Africa, now the press showed all the more interest in pictures of massacres, horrors committed by the civilian population, stories of murder and mayhem. The complete annihilation of political enemies was not just immoral, but inopportune and detrimental to the true cause, development. We told them this and they looked sad, concerned, then went home and wrote more calls to murder and ordered a hundred thousand razor-sharp machetes from Chinese producers.

At the time we believed that those responsible in the military and in the government would lose control of the situation. We were stupid enough to think they were overwhelmed. What we saw looked like chaos, but events were in fact coming under greater control. Everything had been prepared, responsibilities were allocated, duties were assigned, and all the uproar on the surface was just a screen intended as camouflage, sham battles meant to distract us. The ministers complained. They complained that they didn't have enough writing materials, enough money, enough cars, enough telephones. If we just had the means to defend ourselves and to enforce order and stability, they moaned, if only coffee prices didn't keep falling every month, if only the World Bank's structural adjustment program weren't strangling us, if only the international press weren't conspiring against us, if only our President didn't constantly have to travel to New York, Paris, or London, then we would have the chance to reestablish peace and security.

Yes, we believed them and we helped them. We kept giving them whatever they required. They were making a great effort and we wanted to save them. We wanted to give them what they needed to get back on the path of virtue. It is base to drop a friend in his hour of greatest need, and they were our friends. They had been for thirty years. Why should anything have changed? We were righteous people and we wanted to remain so. That meant being steadfast, even though we made it clear to them that our patience would not last forever. We proved this, not by reducing the amount of money we gave them, but by renewing their projects for only one year at a time. Our annual reports were entitled 'A Friendly Nation in Difficulty' and our rectitude required that our efforts increase on a par with their difficulties.

But it was all in vain and the reason for this was the naked fear that gripped us all. And if the fear didn't grip you at first, the endless rants on the radio and at gatherings infected you with it, beat it into you, smothered you. Few of us had any idea of this fear, since we had never experienced it directly, neither had our parents or our grandparents, who had themselves never lived through a war. We didn't understand how seductive fear is. We didn't notice how quickly it spread, because it spread in the Bantu dialect, the language of all the newspapers, political rallies, and radio broadcasts. French was the language of reason and we spoke it during office hours from nine to five, Monday to Friday. The rest of the time, in the evenings and on weekends, this other language took over and I could make out just enough to understand the hatred, the horror, the rabble-rousing. You didn't need to know every word to recognize the alphabet of fear, the obscenities they heaped on their political foes, the visions of horror they painted. I understood the purpose of this other, this new, this unknown language, and that purpose was to spread horror, a horror that etched itself deeper into the people's faces day by day.

I could see this horror etched into Agathe's face as well, in her eyes, which were hardly ever at rest but darted this way and that as if she expected an ambush, an attack from any direction, as if there were traps hidden in every corner of the house. She sought lies and conspiracies everywhere and she found them all around her, in inaccurate reports in *Le Monde,* in the World Bank's unreasonable demands, in the budget cuts of an insignificant Christian relief organization. She didn't know what was happening, she only knew that her extermination had been decreed, along with the extermination of the republic and of democracy, the extermination of her family, the destruction of everything her father had fought for. It was clear to her that the peace negotiations would only lead the country into feudalism, reestablish the aristocracy and destroy all those who opposed it. She stood behind her President, but she also knew he was weak and completely under the sway of his wife and her clan. He was too kind, too trusting, and he didn't know how demonic his enemies were, he couldn't see the extent of their monstrosity, the depth of their malice. He saw them as opponents, not enemies. Even if he occasionally got a bit carried away in his speeches, denouncing the internal enemy as an immediate threat and calling for resistance, these weren't deeply held views, merely a response to the current situation, to the masses boiling with anger. A line of defense, a republican rampart, should be built behind this brave man.

It probably took me so long to notice Agathe's transformation because we saw each other so often and the change was so gradual. On top of that, new developments came rushing in one after the other. Conferences were called and then cancelled. Political parties were formed then dissolved. A week didn't go by without murders – ten men here, three hundred there. Even at the agency we got used to it.

Agathe now wore only traditional clothing. She threw out her capris and tops that left her shoulders bare, along with her high-heeled shoes. She didn't want to be taken for a *femme libre*, for one of the Longs, for an enemy of the republic. It was time to declare one's origins, one's heritage, which one had to defend with all necessary means. She attended rallies for the Coalition for the Defense of the Republic, her brother's new party and the most radical of the many radical parties.

We rarely spent weekends together any more. She no longer let me cook for her. She thought it was childish and inappropriate for her to be sitting on the veranda with a drink. Now and then she showed up at Amsar House on a Sunday evening after the demonstrations had dispersed, exhausted and drenched in sweat, with a thick bundle of political manifestos under her arm, twelve point programs that she studied by candlelight on the porch. She didn't pay me the slightest attention. Naturally, I'd have preferred to talk with her, but when I tried to begin a conversation, she fell silent after a few sentences and the conversation died. Still, this was better than when she did start to talk and treated me to the slogans she'd heard that day, paranoid fantasies she tried to repeat as if they came from her. But the phrases seemed to pass through Agathe like a virus that needs a host organism, using her voice to spread and infect others. *We will not allow the social revolution to be undone! The anarcho-feudalistic element refuses to accept the will of the people expressed in the revolution of 1959 and, above all, in the Kamarampaka Referendum of September 25, 1961!* No one can run around all week with sentences like that rolling out of one's mouth, and then on Sundays suck an *umuzungu's* cock as easy as you please. *You may have colonized our country*, Agathe announced one day, *but I won't let you colonize my body.* That sort of thing. At first I tried to contradict her. I told her that as a Swiss, I had nothing to with colonialism, and besides I thought it was as fun for her as it was for me. She laughed bitterly. I know what fun means for an *umuzungu*, she said, you just humiliate others in the same old ways over and over again.

I went to party rallies with Agathe two or three times, just to spend time with her. Boiling, furious crowds were egged on by demagogy spewing from rattling loudspeakers. These sweat-drenched, drunken, angry crowds repeated rhythmic chants I could not understand, but which were most certainly not advocating peace. Banners called for the end of slavery, of servitude, of disunity, and denounced symbols of the monarchy like the *kalinga,* the King's sacred drum hung with the genitals of conquered enemies and rebels. Long live the republic! Down with the monarchy! No to feudalism! No to *kalinga*! Some carried spears. Afterwards they sang and had grilled meat and warm beer. The rallies were more exciting than any rock concert because they were about matters of life and death. The people there looked at me suspiciously, warily, and I knew that with one wrong word I would be a dead man. It was a hellish sight, a seething cauldron of fear, rage, and alcohol.

Unless you've experienced it, you can't imagine how far desire can go, how cathartic sex can be after this kind of rally, how incredibly healing, how soothing, consoling, how the power of an orgasm can erase, for a few seconds, all contradictions. The contradictions here were enormous, the violence and evil were self-evident, and yet, as soon as Agathe took hold of me, it was all suddenly irrelevant. They're cockroaches, David, and a cockroach can't give birth to a butterfly, she said, and I grabbed her. A Tutsi will always be a Tutsi, she went on, and I slipped off her underwear. They've never changed. Her dress fell to the ground. There's no difference between the cockroaches attacking us now and the cockroaches who oppressed us for years, and I buried my head between her legs. They're murdering, raping, and pillaging now just as they did then. Only then did she finally stop talking.

The sex was never better, never more depraved, never more out of control, never more piggish than it was that night after the rally. It wasn't because of Agathe, but because of me. I couldn't let go of her, all night long I just wanted more. When I woke the next morning and discovered she had already left, to go to mass, my head ached as if I had a hangover. I had no idea what had come over me the night before, what caused my fit. All day long I could only think of Agathe, at least that's what I thought until I realized that what I was obsessing about was not her body, but her beautiful mouth that had spouted such unspeakably vile words and her perfectly shaped head filled with paranoid, militant, and murderous thoughts. I sensed that her opinions and the hellish fuck of the previous night were connected somehow, and I wondered if I was a pervert after all. The following Saturday confirmed my suspicion. Or at least, I learned on that day that sex has less to do with love and harmony than with fighting and subjugation. She appeared unexpectedly in Amsar House. It was still morning and at first I didn't want to let her in because Erneste hadn't finished the housework. I was afraid there might be a conflict between the two. But Agathe wouldn't be put off. She suspected the reason for my reserve, but didn't let it show until she poured herself a glass of milk in the kitchen and a second later dropped it on the floor, where it shattered. Instead of apologizing for her clumsiness, she ordered the housekeeper to clean up the mess. Erneste obeyed silently, without expression, while Agathe stood there insulting her, telling her that cockroaches were finally were they belonged, on the ground. Erneste let it all wash over her as she mopped up. And I just stood there, shocked to realize that something in my trousers was stirring while the milk suddenly began to turn pink. Erneste had cut herself on a shard of glass.

This didn't satisfy Agathe, just the opposite, she became even more furious. I wanted Agathe even more at that moment. She bent over the pitiful Erneste, spittle spraying as she swore. Agathe was filled with hatred, disgust, rage. I had quite literally to pull myself together, to force myself to intervene. I sent Erneste to the bathroom so she could bandage the cut and I swept up the rest of the glass myself. Agathe watched me with a provocative expression on her face, a mixture of triumph, mockery, and scorn. I reprimanded her and tried to explain calmly and clearly that I didn't want to see anything like this again. I told her that in Amsar House, everyone was equal, and so on. I recited the charter of human rights, then Erneste appeared with a bandage on her hand. No sooner had I sent Erneste home than Agathe and I fell on each other and went at it like two hungry animals, breathless and out of our minds. But it was quick. After just a quarter of an hour, I sat there with my trousers open on the sofa, alone, because Agathe had got up right away, dressed calmly, and left. I don't know how long I sat there, I only know that it was dark outside by the time I stood up, knees shaking, and planted myself under a hot shower for ages, until the bathroom filled with steam and the tank was finally empty and only cold water flowed from the shower head. I had the feeling that Erneste's blood was sticking to my skin. I was ashamed and didn't know how I could ever face my housekeeper again. I did not understand how I could desire this devious, sadistic, bigoted little racist. At some point, I fell asleep and awoke to noise in the garden, to Théoneste's voice speaking to his nephew, who occasionally came along on Sundays to give his uncle a hand. When I stepped out in the garden, I saw feathers and down dancing around their heads and thought they were shaking out pillows. But strangely, they were beating the pillows with bamboo sticks. Still groggy with sleep, I went up to them and realized that something was moving at their feet. Then I heard barking and thought they'd caught a jackal. They hunted jackals mercilessly here because they went after the chickens. In Kyovou, a wealthy neighborhood, there were no henhouses. The jackals got into the rich people's rubbish bins, where they could always find something good to eat. More and more feathers were flying, whirling in the air. I called out to them, but they didn't hear. I clapped my hands, yelled, and the two of them turned to face me. Then I saw it. It wasn't a jackal. A buzzard was crouched in a gap in the wall, trying to escape the blows, and as soon as these let up, it rushed out between the men and tried to fly away. It got as high as Théoneste's shoulder before the boy knocked it out of the air. The bird fell to the ground and made a noise that bore no resemblance to a bird's cry. The events of the previous day flashed before me and I started yelling at the man and his nephew, I yelled at the top of my lungs and the two of them shrank back, away from the bird. It was a young buzzard, with a sand-colored breast and dark wings.

At daybreak you saw buzzards in the air over Kigali. They rose, motionless, on currents of air, searching for prey. Buzzards are solitary, they live and hunt alone. Their survival depends on highly developed senses: eyes that can make out a cicada in tall grass at a hundred meters. People believe they bring bad luck. Everything that is wild and untamed, that doesn't lay eggs or let itself be milked, brings bad luck in their eyes, and the best thing to do is to eat this bad luck. The markets in Cyangugu on the Congolese border sold tons of game every day: Duiker antelopes, Cape baboons, and Diadem monkeys, preferably smoked. No one ate buzzards, however. They were the rats of the air, of no economic value, in competition for the same food sources.

I sent the gardener to get one of the baskets he usually used for grass clippings. The bird kept jumping about a meter off the ground, trying to get airborne, but it couldn't manage. We had a hard time catching the bird under the basket. It slashed at our hands with its beak, but once we finally managed to trap it and the buzzard had calmed down somewhat, I was able to take a closer look at its injuries. Its right wing was broken and hung down like a loose sail. I had got there too late, the bird would never fly again. It would have been better off dead. For a moment, I considered leaving the bird to Théoneste, or wringing its neck myself, but when I glanced at the boy I seemed to see bloodlust in his eyes, a pleasure in this creature's suffering, the same dominating, provocative look I had seen in Agathe's eyes. I decided to do whatever was necessary to keep this animal alive, and I didn't care whether or not a quick death would have been easier on it. I wanted to show them how precious life, each individual life, is. They'd see what they had started with their blows. Even if Théoneste was too old to learn this lesson, I could still set his young nephew an example. Of course, I realize how presumptuous it was, but in so far as I could teach this child respect for his fellow creatures, I would be doing my part to end the cycle of violence. I had to begin where I had some kind of influence, and where else did I have a chance to make things better than in my garden and in my house? My conscience was bothering me for not stepping in early enough the day before and I was thankful for the chance to make up for it a little.

I went to the market and bought a chicken cage, cattle bones, and goat liver, which I mixed with raw egg, as my father had taught me when we raised orphaned thrushes. Three or four of the chicks we rescued from the abandoned brood had died in our hands. I knew how slim the chances of success were. People say that someone who doesn't eat much 'eats like a bird,' but in fact birds are eating machines. They can't go more than two days without eating before they die of hunger. I knew what it meant when the bird refused to touch the pap I'd made, and since I couldn't do any more for it than to let it die in freedom, I let it out of the cage. It stayed in the garden. It couldn't make it over the wall with its broken wing. It took its sweet time to die. At night, its cries woke the entire neighborhood, and I could only hope it would starve soon, so I wouldn't have to kill it myself.

Agathe had no sympathy for the bird. What exactly do you want to do with it, she asked one night when its cries woke us both. It will probably die soon, I said, hoping she would put up with its cries until it did. She just grimaced with contempt and demanded I go out and kill the buzzard immediately. I told her that was absolutely out of the question, that I'd already given him a name, Shakatak. She called me a coward, but I didn't care. When the bird had its next screaming fit, Agathe got up and put her clothes on. Even if you're too much of a coward to make that creature stop, I'm not. This scared me, and I held her back. I didn't rescue the bird from the gardener just to let my lover kill it.

Agathe got undressed again and sat her bare bottom on my pillow, which I couldn't stand. To make me even angrier, she lit a cigarette and used my glass as an ashtray. I asked her to stop smoking but she took no notice. She ridiculed my sentimentality, as she called it, a term I never would have used in this situation. You've read too many stories about knights in shining armor, she said. But this thing here is not a falcon, it's a buzzard, and you can't train it. I didn't see what difference that made. We had turned the light on long before and now found ourselves caught up in a discussion that sooner or later was going to end in an argument. You kill flies and mosquitoes, why can't you do the same with this bird, she jeered, just because buzzards have feathers and not compound eyes?

The other Agathe had returned. This was not the Agathe who studied in Brussels, who liked the same music as I did, and who, aside from her skin color, was a lot like me. Now she belonged to another culture. I saw the descendant of African farmers engaged in a constant battle with nature and unable to think past their next meal, or, at the very most, past the next harvest. She considered the bird nothing but a nuisance, an inferior part of creation she could destroy with impunity. For her it was not a sin, quite the contrary, it was necessary to kill the bird. You had to fight to keep it from eating your food and bothering the neighbors. She had no feeling for the buzzard's beauty, the grace of its movements, or its consummate skill in moving through the air.

Agathe took a drag on her cigarette and I saw in her look that she took me for one of those typical decadent Europeans who let cats sleep in their beds and keep rats as house pets. She accepted the bird's death as necessary for a peaceful night's sleep. She seemed not to have the smallest shred of compassion for this suffering creature. No matter how much this repelled me, even frightened me, something about Agathe's lack of empathy attracted me – her coldness, her pragmatism devoid of sympathy and focused only on results. I wanted to know what she was thinking, if she had in her heart even the tiniest grain of love for this creature, because if there was, I needed to cultivate this seed. How could we love each other if I had feelings for something she simply rejected? I thought it would be best to begin with a kiss and pressed my lips against hers. I closed the mouth that said such brutal, heartless things. I was a bit surprised that her tongue wasn't stiff as leather, but still smooth, without barbs, and I kept exploring this soft, delicate, tender and sensitive part of the hardhearted Agathe. The bird screamed, but we didn't hear it.

Week by week I sank deeper into this dark, frightening passion, and when I arrived at the office and listened to Marianne's reasonable, honest ideas about how to solve existing problems, or when we met with a delegation from the Ministry of Planning to discuss increased efforts, better planning, and more efficient execution, I felt like I had dropped into another country, into a parallel universe in which human beings spoke as humans, in which doors looked like doors, and voices sounded like voices. Yet it was all an illusion. It was a new game played by the old rules, even though other laws determined reality. They demanded writing implements and – because pencils aren't evil and you can't do good without them, because every good deed required a pencil, a pencil and a teacher, a telephone and a paved road, because there was no better proof of our loyalty, and because we were obliged by some secret curse to offer ever greater proof of our trustworthiness, and because there was no better proof of this than a graded road, or a telephone ringing for the first time in some remote prefecture, or a sharpened Swiss pencil in the hand of a low-level official – we provided them with pencils, pencils with which they wrote out their death lists. That's why we installed telephones for them, telephones they used to order murders. That's why we built them streets, streets on which the murderers drove to their victims.

We were blinded by our sense of virtue, which commanded us

to help. And I don't believe they betrayed us or tried to pull the wool over our eyes. They just didn't bother us with facts that would have tested our loyalty.

We weren't so stupid that we didn't notice that they were hiding certain things from us, that the assistant bookkeepers and the typists told us one version of the truth and at sundown another version began, a truth told in the native dialect, with intrigues, secret networks, decrees that sounded like repudiations, inexplicable promotions, and apparently arbitrary demotions.

Occasionally I vowed I would tear down the curtain and demolish their world with a single true word, and I sat there in our conference room with the upright officials, small and intimidated in their armchairs, and Marianne next to me, demanding honesty, order, candor, justice. It was all so appealing, so perfectly justified. Marianne was a strict and consummate leader, and the weedy officials in their suits a few sizes too large were so meek and submissive that spoiling this game seemed sacrilegious.

Igihirahiro began. This was 'the period of uncertainty' between the signing of a peace accord that was never implemented and the outbreak of the genocide. In the south of the country, politicians were murdered. In Kigali, one demonstration followed another, each leaving behind a half dozen dead. The leader of the Social Democrats was shot in the head. In Burundi, the first freely elected president was killed by the army. Thousands fled across the border, spreading panic. Things were not looking good, but as for me, I still wanted to see the gorillas in the Virungas. It's difficult to imagine, but in the months after the ceasefire, a sense of normality returned. Even in February 1993, when the rebels renewed their attacks and advanced to the outskirts of Kigali while hundreds of thousands fled from the north seeking refuge in the capital, the social life of the international community continued as usual.

Missland was laying his trails of scrap paper. He chose areas south-east of the city, where he didn't have to worry about running into rebels. In the evening people met in the bars of the Hôtel des Mille Collines or the Diplomate, and you could almost believe the good old days had returned. There were goodbye parties for embassy workers and welcome parties for new development workers. No anniversaries or birthdays were neglected. Although the security situation for the locals was still uncertain, the situation for us, the expats, improved after the peace accord was signed in August, not just externally, but internally as well, because we could convince ourselves that the country was on the path to peace. A multi-party government was going to be established. Refugees were going to be allowed to return. And finally, even the French soldiers and the United Nations' blue helmets, led by the Canadian general with the moustache and the sad eyes, had arrived in Kigali. Only the UN soldiers from Belgium caused trouble. When they weren't demolishing the bar at the Mille Collines, or beating up a political official from Agathe's party, or threatening to kill someone because his newspaper had once again offended Belgium by criticizing Belgian soldiers just because they now and again screwed Tutsi women in their old Bedfords, they drank in the cabarets until they had to be dragged outside, boasted about having killed a few hundred civilians in Somalia, and bragged that they knew how to kick African ass. Agathe hated them. She believed they were part of the conspiracy against her people and in the agency we shook our heads over the fact that the United Nations sent soldiers from a despised colonial power to this country as peacekeepers.

Brussels withdrew all their blue helmets less than two weeks after the President's plane was shot down and the killing began. The Belgians couldn't bear the sight of their ten comrades being killed along with the prime minister. But I've always asked myself what good peacekeepers can possibly do if they serve only as long as none of them are killed. Just one poorly armed contingent remained. When I saw them occasionally during the hundred days, rushing past Amsar House in their ancient transports, I felt sorry for them. They could not intervene, nor could they use their weapons. They were forced to stand by and watch the slaughter, with the result that their gentle, peaceful souls were destroyed.

But back then, in the last great rainy season before the killing started, the sight of their sky-blue helmets encouraged us to resume normal life, and after the months of war, of massacres, when we were stuck in Kigali, we indulged our longing for distraction by convincing ourselves that we had to set an example for the common folk. We should appear confident and courageous, because we were well aware that peace is a delicate flower. We explained away the murders and massacres as the last sparks of a dying flame. And so we started taking weekend trips again, outings to Kivu or on photo safaris in the Akagera National Park, where we counted gnus and laughed at the warthogs.

Whenever you were in a group of, say, six to eight *abazungu,* there was almost always at least one person who had just come back from the Virungas National Park. Surprisingly, very few who had seen the gorillas there wanted to speak about them, although everyone was happy to talk about their adventures in the other nature reserves. But the initiates who had visited the mountain rainforest were instantly recognizable by their blissful smiles, shining eyes, and general inward focus, but they rarely shared their experience and only after gentle insistence. Yes, I saw them, they'd murmur entranced, but that's not important. Then what is important, you might ask, and they'd look at you with contempt and pity because you were not one of the initiates. They saw *me,* they'd answer, they looked into the depths of my soul. And if you persisted, asking what the gorillas had seen there, they'd stop talking and refuse to share their precious experience. They just said, You have to go yourself, drive to Ruhengeri, pay the 4,500 francs and climb up the sides of the volcano.

The gorillas were the kings of this country, its spiritual leaders, something like its zero meridian, the coordinates to which everything refers. Dian Fossey's book was required reading and after her violent death at the hands of poachers, she was considered a saint, a martyr of the Order of the *Gorilla beringei,* the long-haired eastern gorillas, *ingagi* in the native language, the strongest of all great apes, a species native to the volcanoes of Central Africa, hominid inhabitants of the bamboo forests, vegetarian, organized into clans headed by an older male, a silverback almost devoid of aggressiveness, threatened by poachers and slash-and-burn clearing. Their numbers were estimated to be several hundred and I bet that most of the initiated would not hesitate to sacrifice ten, a hundred, maybe even a thousand human lives for one gorilla. Poor, ragged illiterates are a dime a dozen all over the world, but mountain gorillas only live here in the Virungas.

They don't give a shit about the primates, Missland said as we climbed through the last chrysanthemum fields up to the cloud forest. They ridicule us for our love of the apes, and if I were a farmer who had to live in this filth, I'd hate the apes too. The entire world travels to this remote corner of eastern Africa just to stare at their hairy brothers – rich Americans, animal-loving Europeans, film crews, scientists – and not one of them pays any attention to the farmers. That Missland was also one of these people didn't seem to bother him. Besides, the gorillas' life expectancy is measurably higher than that of the men living here. And it's no wonder. The locals don't see any of the money tourism brings in – no schools, no hospitals – it all stays in Kigali. The apes, on the other hand, are pampered like babies. If anyone has a cold, they're not allowed to take part in the expeditions, for fear of infecting the gorillas. Visiting hours are from eleven to eleven-thirty in the morning. That's the only time of the day when they aren't eating. You have to speak quietly. You can't smoke, eat, or drink. Anyone who has to relieve himself has to dig a hole a foot deep.

We passed the last houses. The weather resembled late summer back home in the Alps, cool, windy, and inhospitable. We were already more than two thousand meters above sea level. We were guided by armed rangers, who claimed they carried guns to protect us from the buffaloes that occasionally decided to attack instead of running away. The farmers paused on the side of the road to watch us suspiciously, and I was glad to leave the last terrace behind and dive into the cloud forest. Soon, other creatures were watching us: five-fingered lizards, bumpy-skinned chame-leons, and other chameleons sitting on bright red plants and looking very much like 'ground lions', the meaning of their name. We climbed for an hour through groves of hagenia, tall trees with dentate leaves, interspersed with a species of St Johns wort and bathed in the heady scent of wild fennel and giant celery, as if someone were cooking a giant cauldron of vegetable soup. As the trees grew more spindly as we climbed and were replaced by bushes, light penetrated the mist. I have never seen anything richer in color. Although the only visible color was green, there were thousands of shades of green, every possible nuance within the range of 487 to 566 nanometers, the spectrum of light the human eye perceives as green. No two leaves were the same shade. When we finally reached the bamboo zone, the rangers reminded us to be silent. They, however, began grunting and belching to alert the gorillas to our arrival. Soon we were sitting in a small, sloping clearing, surrounded by a dozen dark-haired trolls, who took notice of us only briefly as if we were simply another troop of apes passing by. They went right back to their daily routine. The younger ones chased each other through the bushes, the females sat in groups and picked lice out of each other's fur.

I don't know how long it took before I, too, was converted. All I remember is that I was standing two meters behind a silverback who was sitting on a small projection and looking out over the plain right at the moment when down below seven children grabbed their jugs to get water from one of the streams. There were six girls between the ages of six and fourteen and a boy of about six. They were just doing their household chores that day as they did every day. The silverback turned towards me with a tired air and for a fraction of a second our eyes met before I could look away, as the rangers had drummed into us. I stood there, frozen, and tried a few grunts and wondered how quickly and discreetly I could disappear. But then I realized that I didn't have the slightest desire to escape. I stood there, rooted to the spot, not out of fear, but out of love, love for this creature and its calm. Just then the children gave the signal that they were on their way, as

128

they always did when leaving the *rugo,* their settlement. They took the path that led up the side of Mount Bisoke, where people were waiting for them, men who had brought a club and a machete as well as some rope. For a long moment I stood there, enchanted by the presence of this Buddha, this mountain man, and I no longer believed that it had been a good idea for evolution to bring us down from the trees. It would have been better if we had remained what we were, if we could win back this peacefulness, serenity, and complete self-abandon in the moment, and no longer have to live in the fear that the children probably also felt when they faced the men, figures with the eternal, smiling face of evil, which hid the men's true intentions and tried to dispel the children's fear. Falsehood, deceit, betrayal – that's what we found when we got rid of our fur and coarse features. Our sophisticated mimicry had but one goal, to conceal our true intentions. The face with which we observed the world observed us too. We believed it was hostile only because we couldn't read it. The ape there, however, he knew what it really was, because this was his face, because he was what he saw and was not alienated from creation as the assassins were, as the children were, as each of us is alienated and alone.

We soon had to leave. Our half hour was up. As we made our way down the mountain, the men murdered the children, the six girls and the little boy. While I was still feeling inspired by my encounter with the wise mountain creature, the men were doing to the girls what men have always done to girls. A few days later the news spread of how the blue helmets had found the children with deep gashes in their heads and purple strangulation marks on their throats. It wasn't just the horror that enraged me, but the glove that the men left next to the childrens' bodies, the kind of glove the rebel army wore. From that point on, no one talked about the slaughtered children any more. The only question discussed was whether cockroaches had in fact committed the atrocity or whether the militia had sacrificed six of their children to turn suspicion on the cockroaches and to be able to avenge their deaths by killing sixty *ibiyitsos,* as they called the Tutsi.

The crime was hidden behind a mask of deception, and no one could say with certainty whether this mask represented the country's true countenance or not. The human cruelty that led to this act could have been accepted, but not the games that were being played with the violated and strangled children. I remembered a conversation I'd had with Missland a few months earlier, in March of 1993, the day that a task force of the International Federation for Human Rights published its report. Certainly from that time on, what was actually going on was clear. The murders in Kibilira and Bugesera were not random outbreaks of violence, but had been organized by the highest echelons.

This country's history is one giant lie, Missland had said, and he made fun of the experts whose report demanded that the President take measures against the death squads. The man from whom they demand action is himself commanding the death squads, Missland explained. These clever men must know there has never been such a thing as one truth in this country. Everyone tells the version of history that suits them and now they believe their own tales. Where this or that group came from, why they are cutting each other's throats, why Dian Fossey was murdered, whether or not the old bag in the President's palace really is a witch, whether or not the Major General's favorite son is growing marijuana, and if so, is he selling it to the French? Who knows what other rumors are making the rounds. To hell with them. These people have twisted their own history so often, they no longer know what or who they are. And all these massacres only serve one purpose: to give them one undeniable truth. There's no clearer fact than a fresh corpse, and here we have hundreds of them. Their desire for incontrovertible facts drives their bloodlust. Don't talk to me about tribalism, ethnic tension, or land scarcity and so on. It's all rot. The European press is up in arms because they can't find a plausible reason for the killing. Why should there be one? I mean, would a good reason make the situation any better? Have your bloodbath, if you must, but first give us an explanation. Those guys in the Balkans with their expulsions and rapes, everyone looked the other way, because there was an idea behind it, Greater-Serbian nationalism, ethnic cleansing, and so on, all of it horrible and horrifying, but still their intentions were clear. Their victims died for a criminal reason, but at least there was a reason, an idea behind it. And at least their victims got a bullet in the head. That's how the intellectual scribblers sitting in their comfortable newsrooms think. They think the assassins in Bugesera are animals because they use machetes. Did anyone call Charlemagne a barbarian because he killed his enemies with axes and spears?

The killings did improve Missland's status at the agency. His little wife, Denise, was a Long, and what the agency had found scandalous for so many years was suddenly appealing. They were desperate to be on the victims' side. In the thirty years that our people had been in this country spreading their mischief, they always viewed the Shorts as discriminated against. They had overthrown the monarchy and dominated the country's politics, but they behaved as if they were still oppressed, as if they still had to liberate themselves from the yoke of the aristocracy. All this pathos about civil society and emancipation, the republic versus the monarchy, was the agency's justification for siding with the Shorts. And now we recognized that we had supported these swine and were desperately looking for the new victims. The agency even invited Missland to Development Day. They probably hoped he'd bring his wife, who would make them look good.

Of course he didn't show. Long, Short, Tutsi, Hutu, Twa – it was all the same to him. The only side he took was the side of nice ass, and he never asked what kind of ass it was, whether her daddy was a fat cat or a shepherd. As a rule, the Longs had nicer asses, but he wouldn't have stuck his dick back in his pants if a passable Hutu ass crossed his path, even though it's not likely a Short would have had anything to do with him. They wouldn't stoop that low. They were too proud. They'd rather let their children starve than be kept by an *umuzungu*.

The worst is the thought that occurred to me again and again in those hundred days and tortures me to this day, the thought that there was some symbiosis between our virtues and their crimes. And when I looked at Missland, that goat of a man who thought only of satisfying his own appetites and wasn't ever guided by reason or morality but only followed his dick, I saw that his dick did give his life direction and led him, in contrast to us, to do some actual good. In April 1994 he got his little Denise and her family out of the country. He didn't do it because he liked her four brothers, three sisters, sixteen cousins and three aunts and uncles. On the contrary, he despised them all and only saved them because he couldn't have Denise's sweet little ass without saving her relatives' fat ones. Denise would never have left her family behind in Kigali, and if Missland wanted to get into her pants again, he had to get them out. He sold everything he owned — his car, his house, and his furniture. There was just enough money to buy thirty-one plane tickets and passports with the required visas. Forty-eight hours after the President's plane was shot down, they were all sitting on a flight to Brussels. This perpetually horny goat of a man, corrupt to the bone and completely unconcerned about his reputation, is the only one of us who gave up everything he owned to save lives. And he didn't save just one life, he saved thirty souls or, to be more exact, twenty-nine souls and one ass.

Little Paul, Marianne and the other expats fled the burning city without once looking back. Their work was done. These people didn't deserve their loyalty. Besides, what good would it do to get a few of them out of the country if you had to leave the majority behind? The best you hope for is to save one or two or maybe even twenty lives among thousands. That's not proof of rectitude, it's pure sentimentality.

In the last days of 1993, just before my fourth Christmas in Kigali, I was on my way to the post office, laden with packages and letters. On Avenue de la Paix, I noticed a frog that had been run over and squashed flat by a car. I remembered that once on my way to Gitarama, a buzzard dived onto some prey less than ten meters in front of my car. I slammed on the brakes and braced myself for the impact, but before the bumper hit it, the bird rose into the air, a dead viper in its talons.

I handed my packages over the counter, and on the way home, I scraped the amphibian, now black with dirt and asphalt, off the road with a pen. I wrapped it in my handkerchief and could hardly wait to get home and offer the buzzard my prey.

The bird hesitated, looked at the frog from all sides and finished it off with a few pecks of its beak. It devoured the carrion in seconds, then begged and screamed for more. So that was what I should bring him. There was only half an hour of daylight left. On African Unity Street I found a dried up gecko, no bigger than my thumb. That was all, too little to satisfy the buzzard. The bird screamed all night long. The frog and the gecko had reawakened its will to live. At dawn I went out, equipped with a pocketknife and a tin for the carrion. I was half way to the school before I finally found a house snake, stinking, yellowish brown, and covered with maggots. It wasn't particularly large, only as long as my forearm, but still relatively fresh. It was enough to quiet the bird for a day and a night, until I could go out for fresh carrion. After a few days, I knew where to go. At the roundabout I always found reptiles that had been run over, and near the market there were rats, killed by the merchants and thrown into the ditch. I hated touching these smelly, furry rodents and only went to the market if I couldn't find prey anywhere else. Sometimes the children helped me look. They led me to the dead animals, but refused to touch them.

These morning sorties were a relaxing change from the agency's growing problems. At the local café, I treated myself to a cup of tea with sweetened condensed milk. The hills were bathed in a peaceful glow. The metal roofs of the huts on the far side of the swamps glittered in the rising sun like a diadem. Often I gathered more than the buzzard could eat in one day. I put the dead animals in the freezer and thawed them as needed.

Shakatak recovered and started gaining weight. After molting, he began to trust the man who brought him delicious things to eat every day. He sat on my hand and let me pet him. He made grinding noises when he was pleased. I fed him with carrion, he thanked me with affection and consoled me in my aggravation with Agathe. I didn't suspect how far I was prepared to go for an animal's favor.

It was one of the young, emaciated dogs that prowled around the Mille Collines hotel. A limousine's bumper had fractured his muzzle. The mutt wasn't killed immediately. It tried, with its front paw, to rub away the pain. The driver, in suit and tie, was probably some ministry official. He rolled down his window, ignored the whimpering dog and quickly checked his fender. I lost sight of the animal, but then saw a thin trail of blood leading into a stand of papyrus that formed a screen around the neighboring property. The dog had crawled under the shrubbery and was still breathing. It snapped at me as I approached. The right side of its skull was fractured and its lower jaw hung down at a grotesque angle, like a drawer that had been pushed in askew. It didn't have long. I left it alone.

After work, I made my way to the crossing with an electric torch. Daylight had disappeared and a solitary streetlamp illuminated Avenue Rusumo. At first, I couldn't find the dog. It had left the papyrus stand. After searching a while, I found it under a bush. I poked it with the torch, it was stiff. I pulled it out from the shrubbery by its hind legs.

Someone spoke and I spun around in alarm. I found myself looking into an old man's face. You rarely saw anyone over fifty in Kigali, but this man was at least sixty years old. His beard was graying and he had a few dead dogs piled in his rickety wheelbarrow. In a cage nearby, a dog with a white spot between its ears writhed and whimpered. It tried to scrape off the rope tied around its muzzle.

The stench of rotting meat filled my nose as he passed. He

glanced at the dog and got ready to sling it on the other carcasses in the wheelbarrow. I spoke to him in Kinyarwanda. The old man was startled. Bad dogs, dirty animals, nothing for you. Not for an *umuzungu*. He blew his nose in his fingers. I'll buy the dog, I told him. What do you want for it? A thousand francs? The carcass collector didn't move. For a thousand you can have that mutt. He pointed at the caged dog. It's alive, but it bites. I want the dead one, I explained. He shook his head. The entire world had gone insane, completely insane. He dropped the dog at my feet. It's already got maggots, he said and took the thousand franc bill. I live down there on Rue Député Kayaku, I said, as he grabbed the dog by its hind legs. In a week I'll need a fresh carcass. Just leave it in front of the red door. I'll put the money in the mailbox.

There was a dead dog in front of my door the next morning, hastily covered with banana leaves. The dog had a rope tied so tightly around its muzzle that it had bitten into its flesh and a white spot glowed between its ears. It was the dog the carcass collector had wanted to sell me first. It had still been alive the day before. I dragged it along the alley to the back of the house. I took a small machete from the garden shed and cut off the dogs' paws and its head, then split the body into two halves. I had thrown the last dog to Shakatak piece by piece, which meant that crows got to it first and chased the buzzard away. I put the sections in a plastic bag, but since they were too big for the freezer, I stashed them behind the generator where it was cool and shady. There were seven pieces, enough for a week, but it was full of maggots the very next day. When the stench of rotting meat hit me, I suddenly realized how far I'd gone. I was chopping up strong, healthy dogs that had been killed so I could feed a crippled bird.

The craziest thing about it was that my work and my life here were governed by a similar principle and I couldn't see anything wrong with it.

In January 1994, there was no longer a functioning government. The officials' salaries were not being paid. Schools were closed. There were no more medicines. Lawlessness and anarchy reigned in Kigali. One day, early in the morning, I was sitting with little Paul on the veranda at Amsar House. I wished he would go home and leave me in peace with his story. It was too loathsome, he was too loathsome, this good man. His shirt was rumpled, the buttons undone, and I saw his flesh, his body. I saw his ribs expand with his breath and the few hairs on his chest. I could see he was sweating. He was frail, like all flesh, and had goosebumps on his sides. I didn't want to see any of this, but for some strange reason he had chosen to unburden himself to me.

It was in the evening, he stammered, when nobody could deny any longer that the Guttanit factory had failed, that the *akazu* had diverted the money, and that nothing remained of those five million Swiss francs. It had disappeared, like all the other millions we've invested in this country. I felt hollow. I felt betrayed. All they did was smile at me and pretend they respected me. I should have gone home, to Ines, but I had to see the faces of these lying, hypocritical creatures. I drove to Le Palmier and drank a beer. When have you ever seen me drink beer in the last four years, David? He laughed and shook his head. I wanted peace and quiet, I wanted to make him stop talking, but Paul went on and I had to listen to his entire story. The waiter brought horseradish, he continued, and I wanted to let him know that I knew how he'd got his job. He got it because he was the little brother or older

137

cousin of someone important. No one in this country ever applied for a position. They have someone type up a perfect curriculum vitae and they fill out applications, but only for show. I started yelling at him, little Paul said. I screamed that he should take his damned horseradish back. I saw him draw back and I thought, this is good, he should feel like shit. I drank another beer and got in my car. I drove around for God knows how long. At some point I came to a roadblock set up by the government troops. They told me I had to turn around because the rebels weren't far. How often have I heard that over the past three years, David, how often? The rebels are here. The rebels are just outside of Kigali. The cockroaches are among us. I haven't seen a single one yet and I'm finally beginning to ask myself if they really do exist or if they are just one of the government's inventions. They've screwed us, David, by every trick in the book they screwed us. Their interest in development was just camouflage, a perfect strategy for being left in peace so that they could secretly observe their traditional customs, their superstitions, their suspicions, their clan economy, the whole damned African mentality. And idiots that we are, we thought it would be enough to clean the farmers up and teach them the alphabet and how to count, enough to turn them into good citizens, independent and critical. But they never had the slightest intention of changing, and all that beautiful money, the millions we threw at the same feet year after year, only served to keep everything the way it always was. I have wasted my life, David, I threw away my best years here. I could forgive myself, but how can I live knowing that I forced Ines to live this life? For her it was a complete sacrifice. She has nothing, just me. My work's meaning had to be enough for us both. She gave me a home. She raised our boys. She built me a fortress. And what for?

How can I explain to her that it was all for nothing and that she gave up her life for a man who was duped? Imagine all we could have done with our lives! With just a tenth of the sacrifices, we could have had a life that was one hundred times better. What should I tell her? That the Guttanit factory is now in the hands of the *akazu,* that madame embezzled all the funds? That our work served a bunch of criminals? I couldn't tell her, not on that night. This realization almost killed me, but it would devastate Ines. You understand, don't you, David? I was silent and wished he wouldn't keep trying to draw me into his rant. Little Paul didn't expect an answer and kept on telling his story. I saw the fear in his eyes when he spoke of the swamps he went into that night. But there was something else, a glint that betrayed Paul's glee at the catastrophe, a sense of malicious pleasure at ripping out the guardrails that had kept his life on the straight and narrow. The ground grew soft, he told me, the wheels kept spinning and it was difficult to move forward. Papyrus plants beat at his windshield. He heard frogs croaking like a cheap carillon. Then men surfaced, dark shapes in the headlights' glare. Anyone else would have been afraid, but for someone like Paul, there was no reason for fear. The President was watching over him. If he gave the word, Paul would be killed without hesitation, but until then no one would dare even to look at Paul sideways. Paul heard distant singing. He said again that he should have gone home, to Ines, to the dinner that was surely waiting for him. But it was still early evening – it was both too early and too late. He got out of his car and walked towards the voices, high male voices raised in song like he'd never heard before. He thought the people here didn't sing, but how they sang that night! Softly, coaxingly, invitingly – *Mbonye inga-nji! Mbonye inga-nji! We welcome you, victorious one! Invincible warrior!*

Look at him for more than one day! Sing and part the clouds, our song will resound until night falls! The sky is without clouds! He has conquered his foes! You will never find a better man! Mbonye inga-nji! Mbonye inga-nji! We welcome you, O victorious one! Paul had the feeling they were singing about him. The heavy mud stuck to his shoes. Everything was damp and slimy and soon he was surrounded by men looking at him without expression, as if he were an animal that had got lost. Aside from the whites of their eyes, he could barely see anything. His eyes weren't suited to this darkness, lit only here and there by burning logs. Someone took him by the hand and the group parted. They led him over planks set across streams towards a house. He saw rats below him and knew that with one false step he would be lying down there with them. The men led him to a dugout lit by a flickering carbide lamp. Men sat on raw boards. There was a sweetish smell of refuse and another odor he didn't recognize. He was ashamed of his neatness. His soap-scrubbed cleanliness glowed indecently in this filth. The men sang. An old man who was missing a forearm led with a phrase, which they repeated, verse by verse, more spoken than sung. Then one of them said in French, we should drink some beer. The millet beer is gone, another said. And a third said, then let's drink Primus. And who's going to pay? Not me, Paul heard them say, one after the other. My wife took all my money. I don't have any either. Me neither. And so it went, around the circle, until it was Paul's turn. He pulled his wallet from his trouser pocket. The men whispered as a boy emerged from the darkness, half-naked, wearing only a pair of tattered sweatpants. They pushed him towards Paul, who handed him a thousand-franc note. The boy grabbed it as if he were trying to catch a fish with his bare hands. Then he disappeared and the men took up the song again. *Nta we*

Ukwanga! Be happy, the boys sing for you, songs of devotion and harmony!
Rejoice, your name is fitting; rejoice with your people, they long to see you
again. Don't worry, no one hates you, no one hates you! Nta we Ukwanga!
Someone handed Paul a skewer of beef tendons rolled up, tough,
and salty. He'd never eaten anything like it. You understand,
David, Paul said with emphasis, as if he were the accused and I a
judge whom he had to convince of his credibility, I had finally
arrived. For the first time in all these years, I had the feeling I was
seeing the true, the stinking, the joyful reality. I had to chew those
tendons forever, then all of a sudden they dissolved in my mouth.
They'd always given us the best cuts, wherever we went, we were
only served filets or now and again the liver, but now I was finally
eating what those who never saw a single franc of our money had
to eat. And they would never see a single franc either. Our money
flowed into the pockets of the rich and here the next generation
and the generation after would all rot in the swamps, eating beef
tendons and drinking sour millet beer with no pleasures other
than their songs and once in a while a case of industrially produced
beer, which the boy brought in along with a bottle of Highlander
whiskey. He had never touched the stuff before and he never
would again, Paul asserted. He'd wanted to keep his distance from
anything that might sully or corrupt him and now he knew that
this was his mistake. He'd wanted to stay clean, untouched by the
chaos, because he had believed that calm and reliability would
spread from him throughout the world. And yet he was the
foreign body around which the chaos gathered, just as hydrogen
sulfide needs a foreign body to form crystals. We made the stew,
David, but we never stirred it. The grease rose to the surface, and
the bottom was burning. He told me how he washed the tendons
down with whiskey, emptied the bottle, and gave the boy more

money. The men laughed, slapped their thighs and took up another song. *Ngwino rukundo – Come, my love, come, cloudless sky. I have made perfume for you and want to sprinkle it on your body and sing tenderly until you are drunk with enchantment. Mbwira rukundo Inzira yose waje – Come, my love, and tell me of your journey. Don't go to the sun. I'm afraid he will convince you not to meet me.* Paul tried to repeat the words, at first hesitantly, then with more and more assurance. The men were happy and suddenly they led a woman into the center of the circle. Not a woman, she was still a young girl, and Paul saw that she must be a Tutsi. He saw the fear in her eyes and could smell her. She smelled of cheap scent like the deodorizer in the toilets at the agency. The man to Paul's right made room. The girl sat next to him and when the boy returned, she drank first from the whiskey bottle, stood up and suddenly began to dance with short, shy steps, modest gestures, barely movements at all. She turned towards Paul and danced for him. She stretched out her hand. He stood up and danced with her. I almost laughed trying to imagine Paul dancing, but he was in no mood for joking. He didn't know how he ended up in the hut, but suddenly he was alone with her, the singing and the darkness. He knew it would be a sin not to dirty himself with this girl, not to take off her filthy skirt and let her take over. *Ngwino rukundo Umpo-berane. Come, my love, kiss me with abandon! Let me delight in the beauty that enchants your face, decorates your body, and makes you my favorite. Ngwino rukundo Ngwino simbi. Come, my love, come, jewel that I love, brighter than the sun, whiter than white, more divine than God, come, my love.* They kept singing and my hands, my breath and my senses followed this rhythm. I didn't need to do anything more than abandon myself to the sounds. I know I should have held my hands over my ears and run away, he said, and for the first time since he'd begun his confession, he seemed to doubt his own words. But I wondered, Paul continued hastily, why I should pass up this particular pleasure. Every one has a woman here. Missland has his women, and the Belgians who drink at Chez Lando every night until closing time, they all have their 'second office,' as they call their lovers. Even you, David, isn't it true, you have your little one. I felt rage rising in me at the thought that he dared put Agathe on the same level as that girl and cast me as an accomplice. Even worse was seeing this Deputy Director, this personification of propriety, modesty, integrity, and selflessness, suddenly at the mercy of his repressed appetites. This man past his prime, with his childlike hands and manicured nails, was hollowed out and eaten away by desires he had always suppressed. The thought of the truckloads of affection his body craved disgusted me. His screaming hunger for sensuality revolted me. What did I do, he asked, why am I being punished like this? For a second I didn't understand what he was talking about until I saw tears welling in his eyes. She infected me, David, that little bitch passed me the virus. There was more surprise than anger in his voice and he sat absolutely still for a moment, as if expecting the final, fatal blow or, perhaps, the opposite, absolution – that I would absolve him of the guilt or tell him it was just a dream. But I did neither. I sat in silence and left him unredeemed. I let him flounder until he pulled himself together somewhat and told me how he had completely suppressed the events of that night, at least until he got sick. I remembered the week when, for the first time, he didn't show up at the agency. We were told he had caught a cold, and that was not entirely a lie. His condition didn't seem very serious, but Ines sent him to the doctor anyway. His high fever worried her. But he didn't go, out of fear and because he was convinced he'd caught the disease.

There is no treatment, he said, and sooner or later I'll die because of a few hours of despair and carelessness. After all, I'm fifty-three years old, that's already ten years more than the average life expectancy in this country, he said, smiling as if he'd won a round despite a very bad hand. But I can't tell Ines, he continued, still smiling, and I suddenly understood why he had chosen me for his confession. For three months, I've turned down Ines' advances and it hasn't been easy. I dragged everything into the mud. She has been a faithful companion, a perfect friend, and I've destroyed it all. I'm afraid I'm not strong enough and that I'll infect her some day, I can't keep rejecting her for ever, David, please. He was begging now and worse than ridiculous. This was a man who lost control because of some alcohol and a singsong, a coward who would rather infect his wife than admit he was not the saintly, selfless development worker she thought he was, that he thought not only about his work, about the progress of future generations, but also, now and then, about a bit of tail on the side. The tragedy of his situation didn't make his attitude any less mortifying. Why was he asking me this? I was closer to him and Ines than anyone else and this alarmed me. He really believed I was his best friend, and I found this frightened me more than his infection. He didn't have anyone else and I thought about whom I would turn to if I were in his situation. I didn't have to think long. I would have turned to little Paul, a man who was a stranger to me, and yet he was the person closest to me here. There was Missland, of course, but he was like quicksilver and wouldn't have listened to me for more than ten minutes straight. I was Paul's best friend and he was mine. He wasn't a good friend by any means, but he was the best there was. And how can you refuse your best friend's request, especially if his wife's health depends on it? I probably would have done it, but it didn't work out that way. Early in April an explosion in the air above Kigali ripped through the night's silence. Someone had shot down the President's plane. All Hell broke loose in Kigali that night, the Hell that lasted one hundred days and then some.

My physicality has always surprised me: that I have to get in my car to go from here to there and that it takes time to get there, and, especially, that all I have to do to keep Paul from finding me is hide behind the generator. I'm here, but invisible. If I stay still and calm my breathing they won't find me.

I smell the diesel and it's so dark that the glowing numbers on my watch are clearly visible. My little crevice is damp and still smells of rotten meat even though I cleared the dogs out some time ago, and I'm afraid that geckos or woodlice will come to keep me company. But all in all, my hiding place is comfortable, almost pleasant. I can lean my back against the wall and look out at the canopy of eucalyptus trees. To pass the time I try to name the birds: the little, inconspicuous one running up and down the thick branch must be a mousebird. I catch a glimpse of a pin-tailed whydah, but the buzzard doesn't tolerate visitors. I whistle for it until it occurs to me that it would be better if the bird didn't know about my hiding place. But it hears my call, cocks its head, and stares at me with its left eye. The buzzard turns, makes a little hop, gets off its perch, settles on a thinner, lower branch, then disappears from what little view I have, a narrow strip between the wall and the metal sheeting. I retreat further into the gap and after a few minutes, when I can neither hear nor see the bird, I relax, lean my head back, and stretch my right leg out straight, even though it could be seen by anyone looking behind the generator.

My ass starts to ache after three hours and I regret having left the wool blanket inside. My corduroys are tight. I figure I'll have to stay here for at least twenty-four hours.

Noon. Now they're gathered in front of the Le Meridien hotel and the second group is meeting at the French school, seventy people in all, men, women, and children. I know the evacuation plan. After all, I'm the one who typed it up and sent it to my countrymen. I don't envy them. I feel nothing but contempt for Paul, Marianne, and all the others fleeing like rats from a sinking ship.

I hear shots, not far away, probably near the cathedral, the popping salvos of French assault rifles. Militias have set up roadblocks all over the city. I saw corpses on my way here from the agency, up on Avenue de l'Armée. At first I thought someone had emptied a bag of old clothes in the gutter. The light was already dim and the pile was big. Then I noticed a bare leg and something that looked like a bone. The militias yelled at me, but after a few unpleasant moments, they finally pulled back the boards studded with nails and waved me through.

By now they'll have noticed my absence. Marianne goes through the list, calling out each name. My name gets no answer. She will send Paul to look for me, of that I'm certain. No one at the agency is better known by the militias than little Paul. They know he works for the Swiss and the Swiss are left in peace.

The garden gate opens. I hear steps on the gravel and someone calling my name.

But I don't answer.

I duck deeper into the gap.

He won't find me, even if it occurs to him to look behind the generator.

David, are you here?

I am here and I'm going to stay here. I'm no coward. I'm not going to take off.

Paul comes closer. I pull back deeper into the shadows. I become one of the shadows. Through the small gap between the generator and the ground, I recognize Paul's feet in his heavy hiking boots.

Then Shakatak calls, from very nearby.

Go away, friend, go back up in the eucalyptus.

But the bird sits on the generator cover. Its talons scrape the metal. It screams three times and I can see the snow-white down on its stomach. The bird must be hungry and looking for its owner, but for some reason it doesn't turn towards the wall. Its tail feathers hang down in the gap – if I stretched out my hand, I could touch them.

Paul comes even closer. He must be standing right by the string you pull to start the generator. He stands on tiptoe to make himself taller.

But something keeps him from looking into the gap.

What stops him is the bird.

Paul swears and claps his hands but the bird won't move. It's protecting me.

Then he's gone. I wait another half an hour and slip out of my hiding place. It's suddenly quiet, almost peaceful. A gust of wind blows through the garden and I don't know what to do next.

Amsar House is dark and cool and I leave the boards on the windows. Sunlight streams through the cracks. Specks of dust glitter. I know they will come one more time and then I'll go with them. Now I know I could stay if I wanted, but the game is over.

I'm here, you can come now!

But no one comes.

Three o'clock. The planes will leave soon.

I get in my car and drive to the embassy. The door is bolted. There's a notice posted on the board. The Swiss embassy is closed indefinitely. Please contact the embassy in Nairobi.

Nairobi, where's Nairobi?

Three guys with machetes spot me. They come towards me. Back in the car. To the airport. Maybe I can still get away from them. The men stand in front of my car. I should just run over them. Why don't I? Why am I stopping? Why am I letting them talk to me?

Get out, one says.

I'm Swiss, I answer.

Get out, he says again.

I have to get to the airport.

Get out now.

I should just run them over so they can end up on the pile, too. They don't deserve anything better.

I get out.

The keys, I hear someone say.

One of them shoves me aside. They get in and drive off, honking and swerving. I watch them go down the avenue.

You've got to get back to Amsar House. You're safe there. It's not far. Down Avenue des Grands Lacs, five cross streets, one roadblock at Rue Mon Juru.

Not a soul in sight, as if I were the only human being in Kigali.

In a few minutes, I'll be in Amsar House.

They've been watching me from a distance, staring at me. What's that noise? What's chattering? Is it my teeth? Stop. But they don't hear, they keep chattering.

They've pulled a few stones from the perimeter wall and laid them on the street. Six men. No, not men, boys. They've been drinking.

One of them comes up to me.

Stop in the name of the law!

He says it as a joke and the others laugh.

I pull out my passport and hold it up.

Swiss, I call out, I'm Swiss.

He stares at me as if he can't understand a single word, then looks at his companions. I walk past him without looking left or right.

Bodies lie in the gutters.

And then my legs decide to run.

For a moment, I think the militiamen are going to follow me, but they just laugh. They haven't often seen a white man run.

I run as fast as I can until I see Amsar House's red door. It's open. Did I not close it?

There is a noise from the porch, as if someone were pushing tables around.

It's Théoneste, piling up boxes.

Monsieur! What are you doing here? Why are you still here?

Yes, why am I here?

They stole my car. I can't get to the airport. I'm going to have to stay here a few days. What's in the boxes?

He doesn't answer.

Well?

Some things I found.

Found where?

Here and there. No one needed them anymore. I thought I could leave them here. Just a few days.

He takes my silence as agreement and nods in thanks.

What are you going to do now, monsieur?

I'll stay here. I'll wait for the next flight.

This is not good, monsieur, not good for you. Bad things are happening, things you shouldn't see.

I've already seen them, Théoneste, I've already seen them.

I'm sorry, monsieur.

It's fine. It's not your fault. Do you have water here?

He shakes his head.

I have to go. It will be dark soon. You should go in the house. Tomorrow, I'll bring water.

He leaves. I make a list of the useful things I have here. Two boxes of matches, Italian ones, not made of wood, but waxed cellulose; six cans of sardines in vegetable oil, a fishing boat with a red wheelhouse on the label; three boxes of cheese crackers, one of them opened; one tin of Heinz Baked Beans; a small can of diesel; a radio; a half bottle of *Les Sources de Karisimbi* mineral water, three weeks old and flat. I turn the kitchen faucet. Air comes out, then two or three drops of stinking, brown liquid. Same thing in the bathroom. There's no electricity in the house. Luckily I have the emergency generator, but I have to conserve the diesel. I'll need to be smart now. I set pans out in the garden. At five, I try to tune in to the German radio station. They don't report anything I don't already know, nothing that can help me in my situation. Hearing voices speaking the familiar language is comforting, but I'm smart and turn the radio off. God knows how long these batteries will have to last. I take a few crackers and sit on the sofa. I take a few sips. The water tastes musty. The lightbulbs get dimmer, then go out, and the long night begins. Théoneste comes with water, beans, and a skewer of meat. He piles up his plunder. I write to Agathe. I pack. I wait. She doesn't come. The plane leaves. I sit on the sofa. I look out into the garden, where night has fallen again. I sit and listen to my heart beat.

As a child, when I sat on the can, I sometimes imagined what it would be like if my city were hit by an atom bomb and the outhouse was the only place safe from the invading Russians. I thought about where I would put my bed, how I could set up a place to write, how I would cook, what provisions I should bring and how many, how I could store them. I was convinced I could last a month, maybe even two. This confidence and my careful planning made me feel good, strong enough to survive the most difficult conditions. But now, in Amsar House, I laughed at my innocence back then. It wasn't the lack of freedom or the feeling of being trapped that made me crazy; it was the isolation. I longed for a familiar chat, a relaxed conversation. When I couldn't stand it any longer, I talked to myself. I didn't listen, of course, until I suddenly became conscious of my voice, like hearing an alarm clock that rings a long time before you're fully awake. It was someone else I was hearing and this someone was locked in Amsar House, Rue Député Kayokou, Kigali, but my identity as David Hohl, to which I was still bound, had nothing to do with the disjointed conversations, the voice, or the body it came from, this body, all seventy-two kilos of flesh, and the fingernails which I obsessively cleaned with the wax matches, since I didn't want the filth from this country on my hands. I felt responsible for this shell, yes, I did, just as I felt responsible for the buzzard hopping about the garden and screaming to be fed. The care and feeding of this body was up to me, but this body wasn't me. Just as this body with the name David Hohl, an administrator working for the Swiss Agency for Development and Cooperation – was this even still true? Was my contract still valid? Would my salary still be paid? – was trapped in this house, so I felt trapped in this body, in this head, in this skeleton, covered with a bit of skin, padded with muscles and fatty tissue. This split was not a good sign, I knew that. Talking to myself was not good. Being locked inside was not good. Being alone was not good. The stench of rotting flesh was not good. Eating next to nothing was not good. Being unable to sleep was not good. I was sure to lose my mind, as everyone around me had lost theirs. Maybe one day I would no longer find my way back into this body, but what sense was there in being sane when I was surrounded by as much insanity as I was now? Reason is dependent on one's conditions, and for the first time I understood what had happened with Agathe over the past four years. She had adapted to her environment so that it wouldn't reject her as a foreign body.

Amsar House was soon filled with the plunder Théoneste stowed there until he could exchange it for cash. There were all sorts of books, writing sets, solar-powered pocket calculators, and a dusty peacock feather he set in a bottle on the service hatch. He wasn't satisfied with this decorating touch, so he hung an iron horseshoe engraved with the message *Good Luck!* above the fireplace. The man reminded me of our old cat, who left the mice he caught on the doormat. Théoneste dragged in enough plunder for an entire thrift shop. Decorative plates with scenes of Paris, a pair of binoculars I sometimes took up to the roof to observe the rebels' positions – all of them possessions of the dead, just as most of the goods in thrift shops belonged to people now dead. But there was a slight difference: the box with board games for the entire family, the ballpoint pen from the space center that can write upside down, the fabric wall calendar embroidered with hunting scenes of the English countryside, the egg piercer, the gold-laminated key chain from the Caisse Commerciale, all of this was the legacy of murdered victims. I let Théoneste know what I thought of his plundering, but he said it was better at least to save the goods. Leaving the things to the termites and the rain wouldn't bring anyone back. The dead didn't need them, but he could buy food with the money, and now he had not only his children to take care of, but me as well. Because I depended on his rations to live, I didn't stop him. Pangs of conscience are easier to bear than pangs of hunger or thirst, and I didn't give a second thought to the fact that I owed my life to a looter.

I suspected he did worse, of course, but I didn't want to admit that, until he arrived at Amsar House late one Saturday afternoon – too late, in fact, to get home before night fell. I was sitting on the veranda and Théoneste appeared out of nowhere in front of me, exhausted, dirty, and breathing heavily, as if he'd fallen from the sky or risen from the ground. He smelled of sweat, beer, and something else I couldn't place. He hadn't brought anything, no food or beer. He stared vacantly and when I spoke to him, he didn't seem to hear. At first I thought something had happened to him, but then, without a word, the man sank to his knees and began to say the Lord's Prayer. Right in the middle, I think it was at 'And give us this day our daily bread,' he loosened his hands and wiped something from his cheek, something that was tickling him, a reddish-white glob. Only then did I see that his shirt was spattered not with dirt but with blood.

Théoneste didn't just loot. He was one of those who showed up on Saturdays to do community work, just as he'd always done. But they weren't digging ditches or mowing the embankment.

He gathered with his neighbors near the main post office and, supplied with machetes and snacks, they went out into the hills and hunted men. I later heard how conscientious they were, how they did this work as carefully as they did their daily jobs. And just as they'd always stopped their drainage work at precisely five o'clock, now they stopped their work as assassins just as punctually. If they had killed the head of the household at five minutes to five, they let the rest of the family live. After all, tomorrow was another day and they had not been asked to work overtime.

During the long hours I sat in Amsar House listening to the radio, using batteries Théoneste had stolen from the dead, I often heard the experts' intelligent commentary. They spoke about the chaos in Kigali, about the Hell that had overcome the country, which was true, without a doubt. But now I know that perfect order rules in a perfect Hell, and sometimes when I look at our country, the balance, the propriety with which everything is done, I remember that they called that country from Hell the Switzerland of Africa, not just because of the mountains and the cows, but also because of the discipline that ruled every aspect of daily life. I know now that genocide is only possible in an organized state, in which everyone knows his place and not even an insignificant bush grows on a random spot and not a single tree is cut down arbitrarily, only because an order to clear the ground was issued, because a decision was entered on a particular form and ratified by the appropriate authority. And sometimes, when I see the gears of this society engage without friction, when I don't hear anything, no grinding or cracking, just the well-oiled gears running smoothly, when I see people accepting it all and obeying orders they've never condoned or questioned, then I ask myself the same question in reverse, might we become the Rwanda of Europe? And I know that if anything prevents this, it's not the way our society is organized, our discipline, or our respect for institutions, nor is it our love for order and routine, quite the contrary. These characteristics are not impediments to mass murder, but necessary conditions.

Evil loves nothing more than the proper implementation of a plan, and in that domain, you have to admit, we are world champions. It's what we are most proud of, the foundation of everything that distinguishes us, and a quality we value so much we brought it to the heart of the dark continent.

I've read the reports on our development work, and I can still hear what little Paul said on the morning of the day they fled as we passed a pile of corpses on Avenue de l'Armée, which I thought was a bundle of old clothes thrown into the gutter until I noticed the flies hovering in a thick, black curtain as if they wanted to shield the dead from view. How could we have been so mistaken, little Paul stammered, two suitcases weighing a total of twenty kilos at his feet – that was the weight limit – one of them filled with a few of his favorite rock samples. How could we have got it so wrong, he kept babbling. The task force mentioned the agency's failure in their balanced, equitable reports. It was no failure, however, because if we were their teachers, they were certainly not bad students. They applied the lessons they learned. They analyzed the situation and worked out a solution, established the necessary conditions, procured the resources, organized the tools, drew up lists, trained personnel, outlined a plan of action, cleaned up the detritus, and they did all this calmly and deliberately, without panic, quickly but without haste. They completed the task as we had shown them, prudently and pragmatically. If they hadn't followed our guidelines, they would never have managed to kill 800,000 people, not in just one hundred days.

I beat Théoneste again and again, and he took it. Then he got up and disappeared without a word. I regretted hitting him as soon as he turned his back to me, because who would bring me food and water now? I had enough water for three or four days, but on the very next day I made the first in a series of mistakes that almost cost me my life. A violent rainstorm set in at noon, a cloudburst that flooded the garden. Within minutes the lawn looked like a rice paddy and I used the opportunity to wash myself in the rainwater, as I'd often done, but this time I used the soap Agathe had bought at the market. Its coconut scent brought her back to me for a moment. I took another handful and rubbed it in my hair for a very long time, then I noticed the rain had stopped.

The clouds parted and I stood there, covered with soap, the butt of the heavens' joke. I rolled around in the wet grass, but that only made things worse. My entire body was covered with a sticky brown mess. Back in the house, I wiped myself as clean as I could, but as soon as the soap was dry, my skin itched like mad. I forced myself not to scratch, but couldn't hold out for long. The relief I got from scratching didn't last long at all before the itching began again, worse than before. I had scratched myself raw with my nails and the soap burned like fire. I only had ten liters of water left. With the monsoon trough shifting southwards, the afternoon downpours were growing weaker. Soon it wouldn't rain at all and I had no idea where I'd get my drinking water. I couldn't afford to waste a drop, but after one sleepless night and a head that felt like it was covered in acid rather than soap, I was such a wreck that I rinsed myself off with drinking water. I wasted two full bottles, an unforgivable mistake.

Théoneste didn't come and it didn't rain. If this continued longer than two more days, I'd have to leave Amsar House to look for water in the city. I was terrified at the prospect, but after thirty-six hours, I was so thirsty that I resolved to venture out on the following day. I didn't have to. Before I could set out, I heard steps, then voices in the driveway. An instant later, six militiamen appeared in my garden. They were young men, almost children, in grotesque costumes. They wore blue and yellow tunic-like *boubous* in their party's colors and had wrapped T-shirts around their heads. They stuck leaves in their belts to show where they were from: banana leaves for those from Kigali and the south, tea branches for those from Gisovu, and twigs from coffee plants for the boys from the east. They looked like they were on their way to Mardi Gras, except for their weapons: machetes and clubs studded with nails. One of them had even got hold of a hand grenade, which he wore on a string around his neck. I recognized one as the boy who was a waiter in Le Palmier. His name was Vince and I knew him as a shy, almost girlish boy who barely said a word. Now he looked like one of the four Horsemen of the Apocalypse, his eyes hidden behind enormous aviator sunglasses and his hair, dyed bright red, blazed like a hand flare. He looked around constantly, God knows what he was searching for – traps, mines, enemies, maybe even the ghosts he himself had woken. His head bobbed back and forth without stopping, like a bird's.

As he was glancing around, I noticed the curtains were billowing in a draft. I realized I'd forgotten to close the door to the veranda. In a few seconds, they would find me. At first, I played with the idea of hiding behind the generator, or rather the idea played with me, darting through my brain and searching for a way out. On their leader's order, the militiamen sat down on the grass and laid their machetes beside them. One of them passed bread around, another a bottle of whiskey and so they lounged and rested and stretched out their tired legs. Only the leader remained standing, casting his eyes around the garden. Now he's going to notice the veranda door, I thought, but he headed to the far end of the garden, dropped his trousers, squatted, and relieved himself under the eucalyptus. He returned to his comrades, fastening his clothes as he walked, and lay down with his hands crossed beneath his head.

I watched the murderers sleeping in my garden. They looked like children in dress-up, resting after a birthday party. They breathed deeply, one of them was even snoring. As I looked at them lying there, so peaceful and innocent, I was overcome by exhaustion. I hadn't felt this tired in a long time and it was strangely comforting. As I lay down on the sofa, I told myself it could all end well – my imprisonment here, the carnage. If only I could sleep deeply, without dreaming, then surely we could find a solution for everything. When I opened my eyes again, a white moon shone down on the empty garden. The militiamen had left behind the bottles, one of them still half-full. The beer tasted bitter and metallic, but it moistened my burning, swollen tongue.

I waited for rain the next day, but it still didn't come. On the following day, around noon, I watched from the roof as heavy, dark clouds gathered over the hills on the far side of the swamps. I prayed for the rains to move in our direction, but by evening only a few drops had fallen. There was only enough rainwater in the pan for half a mouthful. I searched the garden for hidden puddles, for a few drops gathered in the forks of branches or the hollows of leaves. I licked the damp off leaves, ate a banana for what moisture it had. I chewed for a long time, but couldn't force the mash down my throat. My mouth was as dry as if I'd been wandering in the desert for three days. My throat was swollen and my mouth and nose were hot to the touch, but I didn't sweat. My skin was dry and felt powdered. I panted like a dog. I had to sit to keep from passing out. Small, bright rings appeared before my eyes, like the Aztecs' solar disks. They formed chains and glittered like sunshine on the sea. Rivulets fed their dancing molecules into this sea. I also saw the mountain streams in my homeland, and the waves that beat constantly and continuously on the shores of Lake Kivu. I saw all the rainfalls I'd experienced in this country, unlike any rain I'd seen before. Here, the rain didn't fall in drops but in blobs the size of water balloons, and they burst exactly like water balloons when they hit the ground. It was loud, too, as if the sky were slapping the ground. Stately trees bent to breaking point under the onslaught of water. In seconds, streets turned into spill-ways, entire mountainsides became saturated and collapsed into the valleys. Every rain shower was practically a flash flood.

More than once, one of these showers had drenched me to the bone within seconds, and now I felt water dripping from my fore-head, streaming down my nose and trickling like threads into my mouth. I heard the thousands of noises that water makes, how it trickles, plashes, and rushes. In one mad, enchanting hallucin-ation, I saw triads of two hydrogen atoms and one oxygen atom holding hands and dancing joyfully on the stones, rolling over the leaves, and rising into the sky as vapor, like pure souls entering Elysium. I watched them as they joined with other molecules to form a cloud, directly above me, high and white and as if charred at the edges. The wind rose, was that a good sign? I hung out my tongue, like a sweater drying on a windowsill. The cloud changed shape, fused with others into a band that covered three quarters of the sky, puffy and full of promise. And did I feel a drop on my toes or was that an illusion? A thunderclap sounded, but I couldn't tell if it was a storm or a grenade. However, what sounded like raindrops were just steps on the gravel path. The militiamen were back. I didn't stop to think what kind of men were uncorking bottles three meters below me. I only knew that every single cell in my body was screaming for liquid and they had some. I stood, as if guided by remote control, and before my shadow fell on them, I called out Vince's name.

I climbed down the roof of the back porch into the garden. I no longer cared what they might do to me or if they killed me, as long as they first let me drink.

Vince grabbed his club. The others also got up and stood in a half circle behind their leader.

I called his name again. He let his club sink and took off his aviator glasses. I saw troubled eyes clouded by death and alcohol in a face that had something of a newborn about it, but with an old man's features – as if they'd returned from the darkness where they had witnessed a secret, a mystery that the rest of us have forgotten. Still, when he recognized me, Vince turned back for a moment into the boy who served banana soda and meat skewers to the guests and always thanked them tersely but politely for his tips. He offered me his hand, which was cold and childlike, without strength. Without another word, I asked for water and he ran back to his companions. One of them handed him a bottle. As I drank it, I felt the water flow into my dehydrated, salt-saturated cells; I was overcome with gratitude and felt bound to these boys, who no longer seemed like such villains and didn't terrify me anymore. It was as if I had fraternized with the enemy, and the sense that these murderers considered me someone worth giving water to in an emergency filled me with love and self-esteem. They kill so many people, I thought, but for me they have water and friendly words to spare.

I don't think I've ever felt more special and I heard again the announcers of the BBC and Radio France Internationale, who called these boys the worst kind of devils, arsonists, and rapists. I knew that this is exactly what they were. I knew what they'd done just a few hours before and what they'd done over the past weeks, but I still saw them as friends, as brothers, even, as people like me, as my kind. Sure, they committed murder. I had no idea how many dozens of people's blood had stuck to their machetes and clubs. They probably didn't know themselves. But they spared me. More than that, they left me an entire loaf of bread and some sausage and promised to return the next day. They wanted to take care of me, it seemed, as if their consciences bothered them, not because they had murdered, but because they had done it in front of my eyes. They didn't want me to think they were animals with no sense of fellowship. When I was a child, we brought our rabbits to a man who lived in our neighborhood for him to butcher them. He hated the work, but no one else was willing to do it. When I passed his house and saw the skinned rabbits hanging in the shed, he would give me sweets in secret. He didn't want me to think he was a bad man. He complained about those who wanted to eat roast rabbit but left the dirty work to him. And I believed him. Somebody had to kill the rabbits, there was no way around it, and the neighborhood had chosen him. But that didn't mean he didn't have a heart. I ate the sweets, even though they tasted of bribery and atonement, since I felt it was my duty to help this sad butcher bear his burden. He shouldn't feel rejected. That is also why I gave Vince my hand, even though

I cringed at the thought. I didn't want him, mass-murderer that he was, to feel excluded from human society. Maybe he was just playing with me, but I saw gratitude in his eyes. My absolution would make the killing he was forced to do a bit easier. Everyone plays games.

As soon as they'd left and I was alone again, I was ashamed of my thoughts and the friendly feeling a few sips of water had instilled in me for these murderers. Not only were my thoughts corrupt, even my feelings were easily bought, and I looked with horror at the bottle of murky water and the gray, spongy bread for which I had sold myself.

Even my buzzard seemed to be avoiding me. It stayed perched on its branch. When I offered the bird some sausage, it just looked at me with disapproval and made a few discontented sounds. He looked strong, almost well fed, even though I hadn't brought him much. Its wing must have healed. I tried to scare it, to see if it could fly, but it only hopped up and down a few times on the branch.

Something had changed between me and the bird. I suspected it was because the buzzard didn't need me any more, and I hated it for its fickleness, its betrayal. It was a buzzard, of course, and I was just a food source. It couldn't know what friendship was and yet I still felt it had abused and taken advantage of me. I noticed how its feathers shimmered. The dull, livid powder that had covered it was gone. Its plumage shone as it had when I first found it in the garden. It wasn't interested in me. It sat on its branch and gave its cry. It sounded content, cheerful, even jolly, but most of all it sounded *full*. So its wing had to be healed, as unlikely as that seemed. Otherwise it couldn't hunt.

At that moment, the buzzard hopped off its branch and disappeared behind the garden wall. It soon reappeared with a bloody rag in its talons. It took me a while to realize what it was eating. I'd actually recognized it the second I was near enough to the tree. But my brain refused to accept what this piece of meat really was. It ran through several possibilities, trying to find a way out. First chicken leg, then lamb bone, but neither fit this limp, longish piece of meat with a nail at one end. I don't know how long I stood there, staring at the bird – probably only a few seconds, but my brain gave in and admitted the word. It was a finger, a human thumb, to be more exact, and I finally realized what the bird had been eating.

I went into the shed, took the machete, and chopped the bird's head off in one blow. As I struck, it looked at me in surprise. It hadn't counted on this. Its head lay near its feet, but the body twitched for a whole minute, at least that's how long it seemed – I didn't look at my watch. It was rather comical, as if the body wanted to prove it could survive just fine without a head. I was afraid I'd feel dejected, about myself, that is, but the opposite was true. I felt refreshed and completely satisfied, as after a day of work in which every minute is used productively.

I went straight to bed and when I woke, I thought at first that I'd only slept an hour, maybe two. The daylight was the same. I guessed it wasn't later than five o'clock in the evening. When I went out of the house and saw that the blood at the crime scene had dried and was covered by a buzzing black cloud of flies, I realized I had slept through a whole night and a day. At first I was taken aback at the thought of losing control like this – maybe it wasn't just a single day, but perhaps two or more, an entire week, a month, even. When my grogginess cleared, I felt refreshed and completely and utterly relaxed. The relaxation wasn't just muscular, but flooded every inch of my body, even my inner organs. I felt like I was surrounded by air cushions and the fresh breeze that wafted through the garden just then was, for the first time in weeks, devoid of any smell of corpses. It didn't smell sweet, but somewhat sour, full of oxygen, that marvelous gas that smells acidic and is almost a culinary pleasure. I drew this wholesome air into every single cell in my body and then began disposing of every trace left by my actions the previous day.

Some weeks later I heard someone sneaking in through the alley. It was my former gardener, Théoneste, pushing a bicycle. He stood five meters away from me, obviously afraid I would beat him again. He would go again immediately, he said, but he wanted to let me know that he had seen Agathe. She came to his settlement in a pick-up truck with armed men. She stood in the back of the truck with a megaphone and said that the rebels were coming to take over the town. She urged all the residents to flee because it was clear that whoever stayed would be at the cockroaches' mercy, and they would kill everyone who fell into their hands. There were already tens – no, hundreds – of thousands of refugees on their way to Bukavu and Goma, where they were gathering new forces to reconquer the country. The heads of each sector were responsible for the evacuation and everyone had to follow their orders. They roared away to the next street. All morning long he could hear the megaphone squawking.

We're leaving Kigali tomorrow, he said, we've packed what we need. If you want, you can come with us. But I hadn't been listening, I'd been staring at the bicycle. It was a black one-speed Indian bicycle with a padded plank where the baggage rack usually is; I didn't believe it, but over the front light was a turquoise sign with white lettering: *The more you hurry, the sooner you'll be with God*. Where is she? I asked him. She's on her way, right? The bicycle has a flat and you wheeled it here for her since she has so much to carry.

He looked away and wanted to go, but I asked him to stay. I've got whiskey here, I said, have a drink before you go. He was confused, astonished, but he carefully laid the bicycle on the ground and hesitantly, very shyly, he followed me onto the veranda, where I invited him to sit down. He was a polite guest. He took off his jacket and hung it on the back of his chair. A paper fell on the ground, but Théoneste didn't notice it and sat down. I poured out two glasses and asked him if he knew where Agathe was headed, east to Tanzania, or west over the border to the Congo. The *abagetsi,* he said, the top dogs, were all headed west, as far as he had heard. But they weren't going to Goma, they were going further south, to the area around Bukavu. If he could choose, he'd also go to Inera, especially since he had family there. But the Interahamwe, the government-backed militias, had set up a rigorous selection process and anyone who wasn't at least a city official had to go to Goma.

What would happen to his loot, I wanted to know. He shrugged his shoulders and said he wouldn't be able to take it all with him and the market was closed. So the things would have to stay at Amsar House, I said. If it doesn't bother you, he answered. And the bicycle, I asked, surely you're going to take the bicycle, aren't you? I have six children, monsieur, and my wife is expecting a seventh. She'll sit on the bicycle. Did Erneste have to die for this, Théoneste, did she have to die because you wanted her bicycle? And I thought, he's going to pick up his identity card, which had fallen to the ground, his license to kill, his guarantee that he won't

165

be killed himself. You know what she was, monsieur, was his answer, she was an *ibiyitso*, a traitor. I only did what I was ordered to do. Nothing more. What did you do, I asked. He looked at me fixedly. I'm your gardener, monsieur, you know how well I can handle a panga. I've used them since I was a child. All my life I've used one for my daily work. As a boy I chopped wood. When I was bigger I chopped sorghum in the fields and pruned banana trees. My hand knows this tool, it's easy for me, no matter what I do with it. Some of them, especially the younger ones who always want to be something special, let loose with clubs. Not me, I never used a club, what for? They're not suited to the work. Some of them work as fast as they can, like my nephew. He mows a field in one hour and claims he's done. But there are stalks left everywhere. I work slowly but thoroughly and no one has ever told me how to do my work. Each to his own. Some work like goats grazing, some like wild animals. Some work slowly because they're weak, others because they're lazy. Some work slowly because they've gone bad, others work quickly so they'll get home sooner. Some bring their boys with them to the swamps and teach them how to work, the way our fathers taught us to work, by example and imitation. That's what he said. They sent their own children out to kill. They put children in front of their own children, victims their own size. He drank his whiskey. For the first time in my life, I wished a man dead. I told him he would burn in Hell and I was foolish enough to believe this would affect him. He was a good Christian and went to mass every Sunday. That may be true, he said, but what should I do in God's paradise? I'd be there alone. No, not quite, our President is there, but it would be just us two alone with a bunch of blessed Europeans, and I don't want that, you understand, monsieur. What could I talk about with our President? I want to be where my people are, my neighbors, my cousins, my uncles, my wife. And that will be in Hell. There's a saying that Imana, the god of creation, leaves the country during the day, but comes back at night. This day has already lasted one hundred days and we're asking ourselves when will God come home, will it ever be evening? God has forgotten us and until he returns, we have work to do. It's hard work, but you get used to it. You just have to be careful not to look into their eyes when you hit them. They have black eyes and their look is our punishment.

I asked him if he knew how late it was. It must be around five, he said, and he had to go soon. But I held him back and said he should drink one last whiskey with me, just for half an hour. After all, we won't see each other again. He let me talk him into staying and I could feel time passing. My inner voice begged him to bend down and pick up his identity card, but he didn't. Soon after, we heard steps in the alley. Théoneste leapt out of his chair, his eyes wide with fear. Now I knew what he meant about the black eyes. The fear of the dying had washed over him and I didn't know how many of his victims had passed their fear on to him. From the way he stood there and looked around, I guessed there must be dozens. I reassured him, told him, these were friends bringing me food. It felt as if I was calming a condemned animal so it would accept the mortal blow quietly. Look at the ground, I thought. I truly hoped he would. It wouldn't have cost me anything to point out to him the worn piece of paper under his chair, but I felt something like the force of destiny and the conviction that I didn't have the right to intervene, but had to accept everything that followed.

Vince came into the garden, almost joyfully, almost with open arms, followed by his men. The one with the gap in his teeth carried the bloody hindquarters of a freshly slaughtered cow on his back. Vince's smile faded when he saw the gardener, but his expression didn't turn hostile, just completely blank, like a child's awkward drawing. The men set down what they were carrying. Who's this, Vince asked, and before I could answer, Théoneste introduced himself and went up to him. I couldn't understand why he didn't finally pick up his damned identity card instead of rummaging around in his jacket, unable to find anything. Vince kept silent, a dark, terrifying silence into which my gardener shouted his explanation, his origins, his father's name, the village he came from. He declared himself a supporter of the republic. Vince only said, Show me your card, old man. I thought it almost indecent that the mature man lost his countenance in front of this young one, but I said nothing then and nothing when Théoneste asked me to confirm who he was. But what could I say? If he was a Long or a Short, that they could find on his identity card on the ground under the chair. Besides, he didn't ask me, and if you don't ask the question, you don't get an answer. At the time, I didn't see why I should save him, an assassin attacked by assassins, wild animals tearing each other apart. Guilt. I didn't care if I brought guilt on myself. I'd been guilty for a long time now. I just hadn't been able to recognize exactly where my guilt lay. I was guilty of complicity, of not speaking out, of joining with the wrong side, but not much more than that. There wasn't much else to speak of and something burned in me to take on a measure of tangible guilt, something I could actually regret.

Yet I was wrong. I don't regret it. I don't regret that they led the man out – he didn't put up any resistance. The men left the garden as if they were just going out to smoke a cigarette, and that's about how long they were gone. They came back alone, without Théoneste. It seemed to me that he deserved to die as punishment for killing Erneste. In any case, he probably would have died of cholera in the refugee camp, and I know which death I would have preferred: a quick one from a machete blow rather than a slow death from a disease that drains fluids from all one's orifices and doesn't kill in less than three days. Why should I have saved a murderer? Because, to be just, I had to be guilty, and once I was guilty, I felt I was just.

Vince and his companions took me with them. I only had time to pack up my papers. That was it. I did wonder if I should stay and wait until the rebels came. I was pretty sure their intentions were better, more humane. They wanted to stop the genocide. Their troops were more disciplined. They weren't going to behave like the regular army and the militias. In short, with respect to my values, they should be on the same side.

Still, I decided to go with the assassins, with those who filled graves every day, who herded people into churches, threw grenades in with them, and set the churches on fire. I went with the ones who gave their children machetes and set them on other children. I chose the side that had created the biggest bloodbath since 1945 instead of the rebels, from whom I didn't know what I myself could expect. I'd heard about their summary verdicts. Sometimes, when they entered a village where Longs had been butchered, they killed everyone who remained. After all, who-ever wasn't dead, was guilty. Whoever was alive had to be killed. Survival proved one's guilt, and I had survived. The militiamen, however, wouldn't harm me as long as they were more or less coherent, that is, not drunk, and as long as none of them wanted anything from me, money for example, and didn't take me for a Belgian, which was the most important.

So I put on a red shirt with a big white cross. That shirt saved my life, but also caused me a lot of unpleasantness. Sick and desperate people begged me for help, including one toothless old woman who stank unbearably of feces. She demanded food and medicine and I had a hard time shaking her off. She wasn't the only one. Again and again, I had to explain that I was wearing a white cross on a red background, not a red cross on white, therefore I was not an aid worker and so not obliged to save anyone's skin but my own. An *umuzungu* as a refugee was something they simply couldn't imagine.

The militiamen had managed to get hold of a jeep. This was only reassuring because of the blond man sitting on the bonnet with a cocked rifle, ready to shoot anyone who tried to climb on. Nonetheless, it took us three days to cover less than a hundred kilometers. The entire country was on the move. The paranoia inculcated in the population for four years drove them on. Hundreds of thousands left behind their hills and whatever they couldn't carry. The streets were lined with chairs, galvanized-iron cooking pots, and all manner of household items that had become too heavy and so were abandoned by the side of the road. And there were always corpses not far from the road, the bodies of those not strong enough to cope with the strain of fleeing and some who were simply murdered.

We arrived in Inera at the time of day when the sun seems unable to decide if it will set and zigzags drunkenly near the horizon. It was the first refugee camp after Bukavu. It was on a slope, extending for at least two kilometers on both sides of a climbing road. Inera covered an area of about sixty hectares. It was the largest of the three camps, but not the most crowded. More than fifty thousand exhausted, emaciated people vegetated here. Each of them had ten square meters, which was comfortable compared with Adi-Kivu, where there were three people sharing that same space. Dirt paths snaked through the tent city and the inhabitants' status was clear at first sight. The richest could stand up in their tents, the poorest and those too weak to build a tent slept on the ground wrapped in pieces of canvas from the United Nations Organization, Somali-style, as it was called.

The spots on the camp's periphery were the most sought after. Only there could you keep a hen or a duck, and some rented land from the local farmers, though no one was sure if the Congolese would respect the contracts or not, since any kind of commerce was officially forbidden. Anyone who had managed to save a hoe worked in the fields as a day laborer. They were paid in bitter cassava, which was inedible without a long process of preparation. The cassava had to be mashed, cooked, fermented, and then cooked again before it could be sold for any kind of profit. UNO workers had set up the basic infrastructure with a clinic, a hospital, an information center, and distribution centers that handed out food parcels every two weeks.

When we got there, Inera looked like a scene from the early days of industrialization. All the families were cooking at the same time. There was a fire in front of every tent, a miniature factory spewing thick smoke. The camp was enveloped in an acrid cloud that was only bearable if you held a wet cloth over your face.

I spent my first night under the awning of an abandoned barber's stall. I looked out over the camp from my slightly elevated vantage point. The darkness had mercifully covered the ugliness of suffering with a black cloth and it seemed like a pleasant place, an idyll. Each tent was its own little world, a safe harbor illuminated by a diesel or petroleum lamp. But it wasn't peace that reigned over the camp. The whimpering of hungry children came from many tents, and not far from me, under the standpipe awning, lay a woman who had trouble breathing and every now and again gave smothered cries of pain while her hands scratched at the dirt. No, there was no peace, just a world filled with tired, silent people lying down to sleep and waiting for a new day. Their resignation, in such miserable conditions, floored me.

The men checked their tents one last time and made sure the cleats were holding. The women closed the tent flaps punctually at eight and placed their cooking utensils just inside the flap in an improvised alarm system. If anyone tried to enter the tent, the clattering would wake the sleeping owners. I watched the silhouettes dancing on the sides of the tents, a shadow theater, until one by one the lights were extinguished and all that was visible was the moon's thin crescent in the sky. A white man wearing shorts and no shirt, just the vest of a Christian aid society, walked stiffly past, pitcher and toothbrush in hand. He glanced at the groaning woman, then squinted, but couldn't see enough to figure out what was the problem was, so he kept going.

At that moment, I realized how little circumstances can matter. A camp preparing for sleep gives off an undeniable sense of ease, regardless of whether the tents are filled with refugees or boy scouts.

I woke to raindrops pattering above my head. It must have been shortly after six o'clock. The sun had just risen and the camp was already in motion. Men left the camp two by two heading north, each carrying a hoe. They wouldn't be back until evening.

Sleepy aid workers stood around shivering, a cup of coffee in one hand, a cigarette in the other. Two men loaded the young woman onto a stretcher. She had died during the night and I saw that the little bundle they picked up and placed on her corpse was a child whom she had wanted to give life to the night before, but who only caused both their deaths. The men carried off the woman and child with blank expressions, showing neither anger nor grief.

With the morning, the camp lost any semblance of an idyll, partly because I was now observing it with a rested mind, but mostly because of the rain. There were no cesspits and sewage flowed unhindered down the slope, seeped through the tarpaulin, and contaminated the refugees' few possessions with its stinking, fecal stew. It wasn't long before the camp had turned into a putrid, muddy quagmire. The refugees remained calm, only the aid workers ran around feverishly. It was the day the High Commission would be distributing rations, and since I was hungry, I stood in the queue. Instead of giving me rations, however, a young woman pulled me into the tent and asked me which organization I represented. None, I answered, I'm fleeing, too. I came here to eat, not to work. She just grimaced to let me know how inappropriate she found my joke. Then she pushed a clipboard into my hand and told me to check off the rations that had already been handed out. In the blink of an eye, I had been transformed from a refugee into an aid worker.

My task took several hours. Everyone received a daily ration of 1,900 calories in the form of four hundred grams of corn, thirty grams of oil, and forty grams of canned fish. We didn't give the packages to individual families, but to mayors and section heads, and these men, without exception, were the same ones who had led the hundred-day massacre. They, too, had transformed themselves, since the aid organizations considered fleeing murderers as clients in equal need of food, blankets, and shelter. These organizations were not involved in politics, just as our agency had never become involved in politics. Others did that for us, namely the murderers themselves, who rebuilt their state in the camps exactly as it had been. The top dogs were still the top dogs and got their rations first and the biggest tents in the best locations, while the little people got crumbs or whatever was left, for which, of course, they had to pay.

I fed the murderers, which only seemed fair, since they had fed me. I'd only survived thanks to Vince and his gang.

In the evening I sat in the big white tent with the aid workers, who were, as the saying goes, tired but happy. They'd filled empty bellies and for them a belly was a belly. It was their mission, their work. A victim was neither good nor bad, just a victim. We spooned up the thick soup, grateful and happy to have helped those in need. No one spoke until they brought the canned apricots. Over dessert a man in his forties talked about his experiences in the camps near Goma, where he had worked until a few days ago. The conditions, already unbearable, were deteriorating by the day. New refugees arrived every day, every hour, 25,000 each day, and Goma was the worst spot for a camp you could possibly imagine. The ground was an ancient lava field from Mount Nyiragongo. The surface was so hard you couldn't dig latrines with the usual machinery. People relieved themselves wherever they happened to be. There were outbreaks of measles in the camps of Kibumba and Lac Vert, and it was likely that cholera was spreading in Mugunga. A murmur spread through the tent at this news. But it was too soon to be sure about the diseases, too many people were dying and they couldn't determine the causes of death.

There was a cholera outbreak in Peru when I was there, the person sitting across from me announced. I could only tell she was a woman by her voice. If there really is cholera in Goma, then in a few days it will be like a morgue and there won't be anyone who can stop the dying. Silence fell and for a moment it was as if the devil himself were circling the tent, until the man who had first spoken began to talk about vaccines that spoiled in the heat because there was no air conditioning, much less a refrigerated storage space, about the lack of clean water, even though 100,000 liters of water was trucked in from Kenya daily, and about the thousands of children abandoned by their parents. Simply unloading the three cargo planes that landed in Goma every hour was a problem, since there weren't enough forklifts. The supplies had to be unloaded by hand.

The only thing that helped in this situation was the exemplary organization within the refugee camps, even if some of the people who ran the sections were more than dubious. In his section of the Kibumba camp everyone obeyed a young woman who was clearly insane. She had a scar on her lovely face and she walked around like royalty all day long. Everyone called her Madame de Pompadour because she always carried an umbrella and sauntered through all that misery as if she were strolling in the castle grounds. Four militiamen followed her every movement, all of them armed, even though weapons were forbidden in the camp. But no one dared to take their guns away, since the woman had such a reputation that no reasonable person wanted to challenge her. I asked what people said about her, and he told me that nothing definite was known, only that she had led a militia and what *they* had been up to was well known. Was he ever there, I asked him, had he spent a single day of his life east of Lake Kivu, did he see with his own eyes what this woman had been up to, as he put it? When he shook his head and said that it wasn't necessary to see in order to pass judgment on certain situations, I asked him how he could spread such stories and malign people about whom he knew nothing, not how they lived, nor what they'd lived through.

He didn't answer. He fished half an apricot out of the syrup, stuffed it in his mouth, and encouraged me to do the same. I declined and most of those present took this as a declaration of war. They all went off and from then on left me in peace.

I stayed ten more days in Inera. I wanted to regain my strength, to have enough to eat, and to go to bed early. Most of all, I needed money, and I had no idea how to get it. Luck came to my rescue after a few days. I was assigned to handing out empty canisters to the refugees and had to make sure that all the families who didn't yet have one were given a canister. There were few things that people wanted more in the camps than these canisters. A new one cost thirty dollars and I realized that I should leave this business to the *abagetsi*. I found a few top dogs and set up a good deal. I got them canisters which they sold to the poor families. We split the money. No one noticed anything. The aid organizations didn't seem to care as long as things ran smoothly, and obviously none of the poor would dare stand up to the *abagetsi*.

After a week, I had a few hundred dollars and started looking for transportation. I wanted to go north to Goma and I had to hurry, because the news coming from there was getting grimmer every day. Cholera was raging. They said thousands were dying every day. They couldn't be buried in the hard ground, so they were packed in matting and left on the ground, unless they were thrown into the lake, where they contaminated the water. The journalists who were in Inera all headed north and I left the camp one morning in late July with a reporter from the Agence France Press.

A police officer at the Zairian camp found us a car and driver and so we left the relative tranquility of Inera behind and drove to the Hell of Goma. I won't try to describe it. Enough has been written about it and indeed there were armies of journalists in northern Kivu. Television crews filmed the dying and there was no need for the cameramen to search them out. No matter where you looked, you saw people dying. The journalists and the aid workers were tripping over each other, and while there was no camaraderie and interactions in the camp tended to be rather brusque, they all knew how much they depended on each other and went about their business. The aid workers crowded in front of the cameras. Most important for them was getting contributions from donors, and there were no better images imaginable for awakening compassion and revulsion in television audiences, the first step in getting them to open their wallets.

Still, the television crews didn't film everything – not what I saw, not the motionless bodies thrown onto trucks full of corpses, where they revived briefly and tried to climb down the pile of cadavers, stumbled, fell to the ground and finally died. Nor did they show the aid workers who burst into hysterical laughter at this macabre slapstick. They also didn't show the trucks carrying supplies that could find no way into the camp other than driving over the desiccated bodies that cracked under the wheels like burning brushwood.

On top of it all, the Nyiragongo volcano erupted for the first time in seventeen years. It spewed smoke and lava as if Nature wanted to play its part in staging the camp's hellish spectacle. Striking pictures of suffering filled the lead stories on the evening news and overshadowed all other stories of misery. Every aid organization wanted to get a foothold in Goma. They fought over access to this mission and I knew that this almost perfect Hell, the volcano, and the corpses were not the punishment for mass murder, but a necessary precondition for the murderers to be nursed back to health. It was a good trade-off, because all in all no more than twenty or thirty thousand died of those who killed several hundred thousand. They had the good fortune to perish in full view of a shocked world, and one death in front of a rolling camera is worth more than a hundred unwitnessed deaths. Even if the world had known who was dying here and should have surrounded the camp with barbed wire, imprisoned the murderers, and put them on trial, it would never have been done out of love for mankind.

Every morning, on the terrace of the Hôtel des Grands Lacs, the dead were auctioned off. Numbers were sold to the swarming press people. The aid organizations' representatives carried on like carnival barkers, anxious to offer the highest possible victim count, because high numbers in the headlines brought more donations.

I found Agathe in the northern sector of the Mugunga camp with a view of Kivu and Gisenyi, where we had once enjoyed ourselves; that is, I found the person I was told was Agathe. Although I recognized her freckles and her umbrella with the duck's head handle next to the stretcher on which she was fighting to survive, I could barely recognize my love in this person desiccated by cholera. There was little left of the lips I'd been so crazy about, her eyes were two dirty puddles, and her face hollowed down to her skull. The only part of her that was as beautiful as ever, perfect, gleaming, and healthy, were her teeth, now exposed in a terrifying grin. The militiamen in the tent were impatient. They'd been keeping watch for too long, trapped in this tent by Agathe's slow death. I could feel how much they wished she would die so they would be free to leave and get on with the business of surviving. I sensed that they held me responsible for her drawn-out death. As long as I was there, she wouldn't die. I took her hand. It was heavy with the weight of her arm. I knew that a deathbed is no place to indulge in a sense of triumph, and yet I was filled with a powerful feeling of satisfaction when I looked into her eyes and thought I could see a glimmer of astonishment, of wonder, that I was the one at her side in her last few moments. I always told you, I murmured, I always told you. A voice inside me began to rejoice because an unmistakable look of surprise spread over her face, and for the first time I recognized Agathe. I could see behind the mask, behind the mirror of her eyes, in which before I had only ever seen myself, my vanity, my desire, my anger at this country, but could now see something like a soul, a person, a life.

I should have turned and left at that very moment, then I would still be feeling victorious. If I'd left, I would never have had to face the fact that, once again, I'd misread all the signs. I wasn't the cause of her final astonishment. It was death itself that surprised her, because Agathe died at that instant. I can still hear that noise. In fact, I can't get it out of my head, that sound of her tongue clicking against her palate, the sharp sound that frames the beginning and end of my memories of Agathe. The first time, in Brussels airport, she made clear with that clicking how ridiculous she found me. The second time she made the sound simply because death drained all her strength and her tongue simply dropped from the roof of her mouth. Even though she didn't make the sound intentionally at the end, it mocks me still. I can't forget it, because I knew she would be proven right on all fronts. Soon I was waiting at the Goma airstrip, watching a small point on the horizon growing larger and louder. I fell into its lap and it took me back to the land of innocents, and whomever this land takes in is also innocent.

In the years that followed, I tried to avoid any excitement in my life. Only once in a while, when I hear all the intelligent people talk and read all the clever books written about that time, then I look in the index for my name and little Paul's name and for any reference to the Swiss Agency for Development and Co-operation. And when, very rarely, I do find a reference, then the most it says is that we were there, or perhaps it adds that we put more money into that country than into any other. We were lucky that every crime in which the Swiss colluded had a bigger criminal in the picture, who diverted attention away from us and provided us with cover. No, we aren't the ones who direct blood-baths. Others do that. We just swim in them. And we know exactly how to move so that we stay on the surface and don't sink in the red liquid.

After my return to Switzerland, I traveled throughout this country and found only just men, men who know right from wrong, who know what they should do and what they should avoid. Things are good here and now. Snow is good. I only hope they won't remove it immediately with their plows or melt it with salt, which is even worse. Maybe they'll leave it alone for once. Maybe they'll have the heart to hole up in their homes for a time and just watch the snow fall from the sky. I bet they won't.

ABOUT THE TRANSLATOR

TESS LEWIS has translated works by Peter Handke, Alois Hotschnig, Julya Rabinowich, Pascal Bruckner, and Jean-Luc Benoziglio among others. She has been awarded a PEN Translation Fund grant and an NEA Translation Fellowship. She is an Advisory Editor for *The Hudson Review* and writes essays on European Literature for various literary journals.